Also by Sam Gayton

The Snow Merchant
Lilliput

Hercufleas

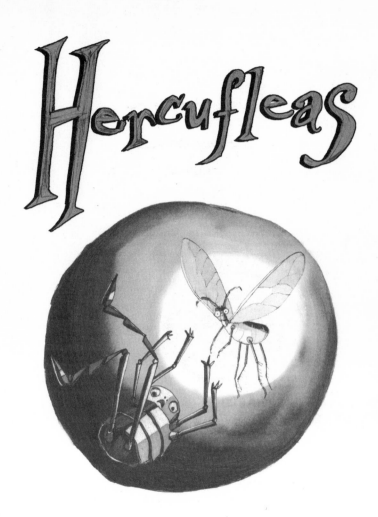

Sam Gayton

Illustrated by Peter Cottrill

Andersen Press • London

First published in 2015 by
Andersen Press Limited
20 Vauxhall Bridge Road
London SW1V 2SA
www.andersenpress.co.uk

2 4 6 8 10 9 7 5 3 1

British Library Cataloguing in Publication Data available.

ISBN 978 1 84939 636 3

Printed and bound in Great Britain by
Clays Limited, Bungay, Suffolk, NR35 1ED

For Rita, both of you

For want of a nail, the shoe was lost . . .
Proverb

Prologue

Greta hurried over the bridge, autumn leaves crunching under her clogs like beetles. The full moon shone in the sky above and wobbled on the water below. She stopped for as long as she dared and stared down at the river's silver ripples, trying to make herself see the past: Mama chopping wood, Wuff with his paws crossed by the fire, Papa stirring soup on the stove. He had told her once about the magic in a full moon's reflection. If you looked long enough, it made a mirror to times long gone. Greta only ever saw her own face stare back. Green-brown eyes, freckles like sawdust, wild brambly hair she never bothered to brush.

She shook her head and blinked until tears rolled down her nose and into the river. It was tradition to cry when crossing the bridge called Two Tears that led to the jetty linking Tumber to the wide world beyond. Her salt mixed with the town's salt, so even though she left, part of her would always be there until she came back. If she made it.

1

Across Two Tears, the trees began and the rows of little boats bumped against each other in the shallows. Greta untethered one and lowered in her axe and satchel, checking over her shoulder each time. No one chased across the bridge after her. On the far side, the town lay empty and dark. Only in the ruined Church of Saint Katerina on the Hill were the tinderlamps lit. Tonight was a good night to be a thief. By the time the funeral ended, Greta would be halfway to Avalon with the florins.

She unfurled her fist to look at them again. Three glittering coins. The last of Tumber's gold.

Slipping her heel from one clog, she tucked the florins one by one under the leather insole for safe keeping. Then, clonking her feet into the boat, she turned to push herself out onto the river.

Tap tap.

Greta froze. At the end of the jetty stood Miss Witz in a black mourning dress, leaning on her cane. The minuscule copper bell hung from her ear on a hoop. A gypsy had charmed it so lies made it ring. When Miss Witz had been her teacher at school, Greta had set the bell chiming many times.

'Those florins are kept in the stone vault below the mayor's house,' Miss Witz said, her walking stick rapping on the wooden boards, 'which can only be unlocked by the golden key he wears on a chain around his neck. They cannot have been easy to steal.'

All the old babushka had to do was shout. The Tumberfolk would come running down from the church and Greta would be caught. But for now Miss Witz's voice was just a whisper. Greta kept her hand on the jetty, feeling the current pulling at the boat, but she did not let go. She did not do anything except sit very still and listen to Miss Witz, the way she had in school.

'I suppose you waited until tonight because the mayor is in the ruined church, mourning with the rest of Tumber. And since he is only wearing black, I imagine he left his key in the hidden drawer of his desk. But you wouldn't know any of that. Unless, of course, you've been spying on him.' She cackled softly. 'And I wouldn't know any of it either. Unless, of course, *I've* been spying on *you*.'

As she spoke, Miss Witz hobbled closer. Her hair was like a roll of chicken wire and her eyes shone the same steely colour.

'So I suppose what I want to know first,' said Miss Witz, 'is where you are going with all that gold.'

'What gold?' Greta said.

The copper bell gave a tinkle. Miss Witz raised her eyebrows that were drawn on with charcoal and gave Greta a very long stare that seemed to say, *And now the truth, please.*

Greta felt her cheeks go hot. 'I'm not stealing it.' The copper bell rang again. 'Well, I am stealing it, but for good reason, miss. I'm going to Avalon, to buy Tumber another hero.'

'The mayor chooses which heroes will guard us,' said Miss Witz. 'Not you.'

'The mayor chooses wrong,' Greta blurted.

Miss Witz frowned, but this time the copper bell did not ring. She half smiled. 'So you believe what you say. But that does not mean you are right. It means you are either a very astute girl, or a fool.'

'I tried telling him,' Greta said, 'but he doesn't listen. The heroes he brings back—'

'Are the strongest in all Avalon, child. And the strongest in Avalon are the strongest in the world.'

'We don't *need* the strongest,' said Greta. Why was she the only one who understood? 'It isn't about being strong. Papa was strong. Mama was stronger. But the strongest will always be Yuk.'

At the sound of his name, Miss Witz flinched. She

looked away, pulling at a wispy hair on her chin.

'Remember the Crimson Knight?' Greta said quietly. 'With his sword of boiling lava? Yuk guzzled him, then used his sword as a toothpick. Remember the Stone Golem, chiselled from granite and brought to life with alchemy? Yuk crushed him into gravel with his heel.'

In the Church of Saint Katerina on the Hill, the mourning bell began to toll from the broken spire. It rang once for every life Yuk had taken. Greta sat in the boat, counting each faint chime. On and on the bell went. Even when the tolling ended, Greta knew it had not. It would never end. Next month when the moon was new Yuk would come again – and only one thing could stop him.

'Every month that passes, there are fewer of us left,' Greta said. 'Fewer florins. A little less hope. It has to be me who goes to Avalon. Tumber doesn't need a *strong* hero, it needs a *giant-slayer.*'

Miss Witz snorted. 'What a ridiculous idea.'

But Greta smiled, because below her teacher's words, she heard the tintinnabulation of the copper bell.

'You believe me too—'

'*Enough*, child,' snapped Miss Witz. 'You are being very foolish. And making me very ashamed. Who was

5

it that taught you to steal in this way? Not I.'

Greta scowled.

'You were clever in taking the florins,' Miss Witz continued, coming right up to the boat, 'but you did not think through your escape.'

She twisted the fox-head handle of her walking stick. With a click, a small silver tongue sprang from its mouth: a hidden blade. 'Did you think no one would come for you when your thieving was discovered?'

Before Greta could move, Miss Witz stabbed the cane down, slicing the ropes tethering all the other boats to the jetty. With sharp kicks, she sent each one spinning in lazy circles across the river, where the current took hold and swept them away.

'How will the mayor chase after you now?' With a wink, she tapped her cane on Greta's hand that still gripped tight to the jetty. 'You can let go now, child.'

Greta looked up at her teacher, searching for words.

'You are right,' Miss Witz said. 'Go to Avalon. Go. Bring us the hero we need.'

'I will,' she whispered. 'I promise.'

'I did not see you,' Miss Witz said, her copper bell tinkling mischievously. 'I was not here.'

Then Greta pushed out on the river, paddling

downstream with clumsy strokes, carrying the last of Tumber's gold, and the last of its hope.

Towards Avalon, the island of heroes.

To bring back a giant-slayer.

1

It was no ordinary top hat. It was tall, made of stiff black velvet, with a red silk band above the brim. And sticking out the top was a tiny chimney. The chimney was made of miniature red bricks, stacked tall as a little finger. On frosty nights, smoke wafted up from the flue, hanging over the top hat in grey wisps.

Below the chimney were three rows of square windows. During the day, black velvet shutters kept the windows hidden, but in the evenings the shutters were drawn back. Then the inside of the house-hat lit up with a warm and cosy glow from flickering candles no thicker than matchsticks, and through the windows could be seen the silhouettes of furniture, the glimmer of tiny fireplaces and the flitting, shadowy shapes of the fleas that lived there.

There were twelve of them in all: the biggest, rarest fleas in the world. They looked just like raisins – raisins with extra-long folded-up legs, and squashed little heads with twinkling eyes, and mouths filled with pointy teeth.

All their short lives, the fleamily (just like a family, only smaller and jumpier) had resided together in their fabulous house-hat. There was Min the mummy flea, Pin the daddy flea and their four sons, Burp, Slurp, Speck and Fleck, and their five daughters Itch, Titch, Tittle, Dot and Jot.

Min, Pin, Burp, Slurp, Speck, Fleck, Itch, Titch, Tittle, Dot and Jot.

And of course there was Egg too.

Who was just about to hatch.

'Can't wait to have a new sister!' Dot cried, hopping around the kitchen.

Burp and Slurp rolled their eyes. 'Egg's not a girl!' they said together.

'Yes, she is!'

'No, he isn't!'

Dot turned to the little fluff of cotton wool where Egg sat by the stove to keep warm. 'Yes, you are,' she whispered, 'aren't you, Egg?'

There in the nest, Egg sat – small, yellow and hard like a rice crispy.

And wobbled.

Dot blinked. 'See that?' she said, wide-eyed. 'I asked Egg, and she just *nodded*! She is a girl!'

Burp and Slurp stared open-mouthed for a moment, then glanced at each other. 'Egg wasn't nodding,' they hissed back. 'He was shaking his head!'

'She never, she nodded!'

'He shook his head!'

'She doesn't even have a head!'

Egg wobbled again. Crack! A thin black line scribbled down its shell from top to bottom. The three fleas jumped so high they thumped their heads on the ceiling. When they landed, they stopped squabbling. Finally they could agree on something.

'Egg's hatching!' they shouted together. 'Egg's hatching!'

At once, Min and Pin hurtled in through the door, followed by everyone else. Egg cracked again and again, as two long and powerful legs burst from the bottom. Tiny flakes of shell skittered and bounced across the kitchen's pebble floor.

11

The whole fleamily watched as Egg stood up, teetering on new feet, legs crouched ... and leaped into the air.

'*Watch out!*' yelled Min.

The fleamily dived beneath the playing card on matchstick legs they used as a table. Egg ricocheted around the room like a bullet, slamming against windows and walls, knocking over chairs, clattering into the thimble pots and pans.

Min and Pin hugged each other with pride at their hatchling's first jumps, while bits of shell and plaster rained down onto the floor around them.

With a hollow *thunk,* the commotion stopped.

The fleamily crept from under the table to find a little hatchling flea stuck headfirst in one of the thimble pots on the stove, legs kicking in the air.

Grabbing hold of one foot each, Min and Pin gave the little flea a yank. With the sound a wine bottle makes when the cork comes out, the hatchling popped free and landed on the table, blinking and grinning at the ceiling.

12

The fleamily crowded round. Burp and Slurp elbowed each other, and Dot gave a sigh of disappointment: the newest member of the fleamily was indeed a new brother, not a sister.

'Hello, little one,' said Min, very slowly and carefully. 'I am your Min. This is your Pin. These are your brothers, Burp, Slurp, Speck and Fleck. These are your sisters, Itch, Titch, Tittle, Dot and Jot . . . We are your fleamily.'

Everyone waved.

The little flea looked at them shyly. He waved back. Then he stared at his hand in amazement and made it wave again. 'So *that's* what waving looks like,' he said, then gasped and said crossly, 'Oh no, I just spoke my first word, and it was "so"! "So" is so boring! I wanted it to be a really interesting word. Like nunchucks, or gazebo, or conker . . .' He stamped his foot in a tantrum.

(Any human readers might find it strange that baby fleas can talk. But newborn fleas are not really babies at all. Inside their egg, they have spent a great deal of time listening to the world outside. And because their shells are strong but very thin, unhatched fleas hear their fleamily talking for months and months and quickly learn how to speak themselves.)

'Never mind about your first word, little one,' said Min gently. 'How about we give you a name, to cheer you up?'

'Call him Tot,' said Jot.

'Call him Little,' said Tittle.

'Call him Peck,' said Fleck.

'But I've already got a name,' said the hatchling, and it was the truth. Inside his egg, he'd wondered about many things: mostly questions he could not answer until after he hatched, like 'What does red look like?' and 'Do I like hugs?' and 'What happens on Tuesdays?' But he hadn't ever wondered about his name. Not once.

'You already have a name?' Min repeated in astonishment. 'Where did you get that from?'

The little flea shrugged. He'd just always known it, as if it was floating around inside the egg before he even got there.

'Well?' Pin leaned close. 'What is it?'

The little flea smiled, because this would be the first time he would say it out loud.

'I'm Hercufleas!'

2

The fleamily gawped at the little flea, then at each other, in amazement.

'Hercufleas?' repeated Speck.

'Hercufleas?!!' Fleck echoed.

'What sort of a name is *Hercufleas*?' scoffed Burp.

Titch, Tittle and Dot shook their heads.

'Can't you pick another name?'

'Something a little smaller?'

'Something flea-sized?'

But Min told them all to shush. Scooping Hercufleas into her arms, she gave him a gentle nip on his cheek. 'I think it's a *wonderful* name,' she told him.

'All right, all right!' Pin laughed. 'Hercufleas it is.' Bounding over the table, he hugged the little hatchling too. 'Welcome to the fleamily.'

'Hooray!' everyone shouted, bundling forward and joining in the cuddle.

In the centre, Hercufleas closed his eyes and snuggled into Min's arms. He still didn't know what red looked like or what happened on Tuesdays, but he knew he liked hugs. Especially from his fleamily.

'Let's give him the tour!' cried Fleck, and everyone cheered and nodded.

'Show him the living room!'

'Show him the boingy-boing room!'

'Show him the cellar!'

'Well, little one?' Min murmured in his ear. 'Where would you like to go?'

Hercufleas smiled again, because that was the second thing he had never wondered about. It wasn't just his name he knew: it was something much more important, and far harder to explain.

He knew *why* he'd hatched.

What his purpose was.

His destiny.

'I want to go on an *adventure*!' Hercufleas cried, and hopping out from the hug he jumped towards the house-hat's front door.

'Now wait just a moment!' laughed Min, bounding

over and tugging him back. 'You can't go outside yet, Hercufleas.'

Hercufleas looked up crossly. 'Why not?'

'Because you're only three minutes old,' she replied, 'and you haven't even seen the house-hat yet. If you want to go on an adventure, you should probably start *in here* before you go *out there*.'

Hercufleas thought about it. 'I suppose that does make sense,' he said eventually.

With a cheer the fleamily seized hold of him, and before he knew it, Hercufleas was whooshing out of the kitchen to explore the house-hat. His fleamily took him down a hallway and up a staircase, where stamps showing princesses and dukes were licked to the wall like portraits. Hercufleas jumped when he saw the last one on the landing: a ferocious bearded man with smouldering eyes and an iron crown on his head.

'That's the Czar,' said Tittle in a spooky voice. 'He ruled Petrossia, the land to the north, years and years ago. Nothing left of him now but dusty bones, ruined castles and creepy portraits . . .'

'Stop scaring your baby brother,' scolded Min.

'I'm not scared!' Hercufleas insisted, hopping away from the Czar as fast as he could.

'Look here, Hercufleas.' Min opened the door halfway up the stairs. 'This is where we sleep.'

Inside the bedroom were a dozen matchbox beds, spaced around the curved wall like the numbers on a clock. On the headboard of the smallest bed, Pin wrote 'Hercufleas' with an eyelash dipped in ink. Hercufleas liked his bed very much, with its mattress stuffed with mouse hairs and quilt of woven silk and feathers, but he was eager to explore more of the house-hat, so off they went again.

His fleamily rushed him up to the top floor, to a living room with twelve comfy armchairs and polka-dot wallpaper. Behind another door was a bathroom with a tin cup raised above a candle nub that turned the water hot.

'We relax in there,' said Itch. 'We wash in here . . .'

'And up this way,' said Pin, leading Hercufleas up a straw ladder to the attic, 'is where we have *fun*.'

Up in the house-hat's highest room, all the walls were made from glued-together elastic bands. There the fleamily bounced and whizzed like a dozen balls inside a lottery machine. They called it the boingy-boing room, and it was their second favourite room of all.

'Whoooooooooohoooooooooo!' Hercufleas yelled,

hurtling from one wall to the next. He landed by the door and looked up at Min with an enormous grin on his face.

'Well?' she said. 'Why don't you go boingy-boing some more?'

'We'll teach you how to do star jumps!' said Tittle.

'And somersaults!' said Itch.

'And when you're *really* good, the double-pike-cross-split-topsy-turvy manoeuvre!' said Jot.

A long, loud gurgling echoed around the boingy-boing room.

'Did you hear that?' Hercufleas said. 'My tummy just said its first word. What does *gurgle-gurgle-glog-glog* mean?'

'It means you're hungry,' said Min. 'Come back down to the kitchen.'

Hercufleas shook his head stubbornly. 'I've already explored there,' he said. 'I want to go somewhere new.'

'Trust us.' Min laughed. 'You've explored nearly all the house-hat . . . But we've saved the best bit until last.'

'You mean there's something even better than going boingy-boing?' Hercufleas said breathlessly as they hopped back downstairs. 'What is it?'

Min smiled. 'It's called dinner,' she said.

3

While Min and Pin set the table, Hercufleas followed the others down to the kitchen's cellar and squeezed inside. With silent awe, he stared up at the racks of bottles, tiny as dewdrops, each one filled with a red bead of the world's rarest, most exquisite blood.

He hopped up and down the shelves, reading labels. There was dodo blood, rhino blood, platypus, narwhal and manatee blood. Blood the colour of crimson and scarlet and ruby and vermilion and puce and maroon. Now Hercufleas knew what red looked like. It looked . . . *delicious*.

(Unless you are a flea yourself – or a vampire, or a head louse – then the idea of having blood for dinner is probably making you queasy. But imagine you are a flea, and suddenly blood becomes the yummiest thing in the world:

like flies to a spider or cabbage to a slug or espresso coffee to a grown-up. Just because you or I might shudder at the very thought of gobbling such things, there will always be some strange creature out there who finds it tasty.)

Hercufleas wandered around the shelves, wondering which blood to pick. No two drops tasted alike, the others told him. Squirrel blood was nutty, dragon blood was fiery, sloth blood helped the fleas sleep and cheetah blood made them very untrustworthy at cards. There was even a drop of reindeer blood, sent over from Laplönd, which Min saved for festive occasions.

His brothers and sisters bustled around him, gathering what they wanted.

'Hey, Slurp, let's have hyena blood again. It's a good giggle!'

'Titch, how about we all drink chameleon blood, then play hide-and-seek later?'

Hercufleas was bewildered. So many flavours to explore! He didn't know where to start. The others began clamouring for him to hurry up, so finally he snatched a bottle at random and hopped back to the kitchen table.

Before they ate, Min made the whole fleamily recite a prayer to remind them how wonderful their life was, and how fortunate they were that they did not have to live like other fleas, who were the size of poppy seeds, and had to survive on hosts that did not want them there, and lived under the constant peril of thumbs and soapy baths and flea powder. The prayer was called *The Plea of the Flea*, and now she taught it to Hercufleas:

> *The plea of the flea*
> *And the tick and the nit*
> *Is to hop in hope*
> *And only bite a bit.*
> *Run from their fingers*
> *Run from their thumbs*
> *And we'll all jump to fleaven*
> *When our last jump comes.*

'What's fleaven?' Hercufleas asked.

'The heaven that fleas and all other insects go to after our short lives are through,' Min answered. 'All the great and good bugs of the world go there, including Pinocchio's cricket and Anansi the spider. Now then. Let's say it together, shall we?'

The fleamily rushed through the prayer, then reached out and unstoppered their bottles. At once an indescribably delicious smell oozed into the kitchen.

Hercufleas seized up his bead of blood and glug-glug-glugged it down. His belly's growl became a purr. A wonderful fiery feeling spread through his body. He felt proud. Brave. Not like a flea at all. He was a *CHAMPION!*

Before he knew what he was doing, Hercufleas leaped onto the table and roared, 'Whatever size his enemies, the winner's always HERCUFLEAS!'

Everyone stared at him. Dot began to giggle. Hercufleas gave her a haughty sniff, but suddenly his courage and pride all drained away. Why had he done that? Blood flushed from his belly up to his face as the rest of the fleamily laughed.

'Looks like Hercufleas has a taste for *lion* blood!' Pin chuckled, leaning forward and reading the label on his bottle.

Min pulled him back down into his seat. 'Fleas can only keep breathing and bouncing so long as they have blood,' she explained. 'But be careful, Hercufleas: you are what you eat. The blood you drink becomes part of you, and changes you too. That drop of lion blood . . .'

'Made me feel like a lion!' Hercufleas cried, suddenly understanding where his urge to pounce and roar had come from.

'Happens to us all,' grinned Burp. 'Last week I drank

three drops of bat blood. Now I wake in the mornings hanging upside down inside the chimney!'

'Blood isn't just food to us fleas,' said Pin, when everyone had stopped laughing. 'It's *alchemy*.'

Now dinner was done Hercufleas sat back, sighing contentedly, his body fat and pink. Around him, his fleamily did the same. They no longer looked like shrivelled sultanas, but a bunch of juicy grapes. Pin and Min muttered silly things like: 'What a fine vintage that was, bottled fresh from the vein!' and 'Yes, the subtle hints of plasma perfectly complement the initial flavours of iron.'

'Where are we going on an adventure next?' Hercufleas cried, but the fleamily were yawning and slumped in their chairs, and Min said it was time for bed.

4

Hercufleas didn't want to go to bed. He had only been alive for Today so far – Tomorrow was an impossibly long time to wait for more adventures.

'I want to *explore!*' he whinged. 'I don't even know what's outside the house-hat.'

'You shall,' said Min. Ushering him into the bedroom, she tucked him up in his silk and feather quilt. Then, snuffing out the lights one by one, she told the fleas a story, which was an adventure you went on inside your imagination. Burp and Slurp wanted a tale about the Bögenmann, but Min said it was too scary for little fleas only one day old.

Instead she told them about a talking cricket and a wooden puppet called Pinocchio. She stopped at the bit where Geppetto the carpenter is thrown into prison, promising to tell the rest of the tale another night. Then she fetched her leggolin, which was like a violin, only played with her feet. In the golden light from the doorway, she played the fleamily beautiful melodies too high for human ears to hear, until dreams came and took them off to sleep one by one.

All except for Hercufleas.

Long after the lights went out he lay in his bed, listening to everyone around him mutter and snore. He tried not to fidget and to keep his eyes closed, but it was impossible. His legs twitched, kicking off the covers. He sat up and looked at the door.

Quietly he slid out of bed. Tiptoeing past his parents, he groped for the door. It closed behind him with a *click*, and Hercufleas was out in the corridor.

The house-hat was different in the dark. Like it belonged not to the fleamily any more, but to someone else, someone living among the shadows in stillness and hush, who glared from the dark every time Hercufleas made a floorboard creak. His skin prickled and his heart skittered and his legs jittered with each jump. Inside his egg it had been dark, but not dark like this. Not endless and swallowing and chill.

He stumbled up the stairs, almost shrieking when he

came face to face again with the Czar, glaring from his stamp above the banister. He groped around the living room, stubbing his toe on an armchair.

'Ow ow ow!' He hopped around the room in agony, holding his foot. He tripped on an armchair, slid across a rug and crash! *Whoompf!* He was in the fireplace.

Ash and soot flew up in a choking blizzard. Coughing and spluttering, Hercufleas leaped from the hearth, reached for the heavy velvet curtains, pulled up the window, unlatched the shutters and gulped a deep breath of clean air.

Outside, there was a monster.

Its head was the size of the whole house-hat, with pale skin speckled like an eggshell, and odd-coloured eyes – one green, one brown. Its hair was a tangled mess. A hideously big mouth twisted into a scowl, with rows of square white teeth, each as big as Hercufleas. The glass buzzed in the window frame, and there was a rumble like thunder as the monster's mouth started to move.

'Three florins,' it said. 'That's all I've got.'

Hercufleas jumped so high he banged his head on the ceiling. He landed back on the floor, tiny heart thrumming with terror, yelling, 'Giant! Giant! There's a huge monster outside!' He latched the shutters, wrenched

27

down the window, shut the curtains and hid behind an armchair.

TAP TAP TAP, went something on the window. The whole house-hat wobbled and shook and Hercufleas trembled.

The giant wanted to come in.

'Hercufleas?' Min called from the downstairs corridor. 'Where have you got to? What's all this shouting?'

TAP TAP TAP, went the monster on the window again. This time Hercufleas stood up. The giant had already seen him, but there was still hope for his fleamily. He was done for, but they might still get away.

'Run!' Hercufleas yelled downstairs. 'Everybody, run. I'll be the decoy!'

Without waiting for a reply, he bounded to the curtains and threw them open once more. On the other side of the window, an enormous finger tapped on the glass with a dirty nail. Hercufleas pulled up the window, trying to remember the courage he'd felt after drinking the lion's blood. He leaped from the house-hat, landed on the fingertip and bit it as hard as he could.

There was a deafening yelp as the giant's blood filled his mouth. It was bitter and fiery and it made Hercufleas feel hollow inside. The giant's other hand flicked him into the air, knocking the breath from his lungs. He fell, bouncing on the floor and skidding to a stop.

He lay dazed, hearing shouts and curses all around. He hoped his fleamily had escaped. He hoped he'd saved them.

Looking up, the enormous pink hand was coming towards him. He closed his eyes and his life flashed before him, which took about a nanosecond. He waited for the enormous thumb to squish him flat . . .

Here lies Hercufleas, he thought. *He liked hugs from his fleamily and going boingy-boing. But he never found out what happened on Tuesdays . . .*

The giant didn't squash him. It plucked him up, dangling him in the air.

'Can I have this, but in a bigger size?' it said.

5

Hercufleas was at the kitchen table, sipping koala blood to calm him down. Min gave him another hug and a nip on the cheek. Pin was outside, smoothing things over with the monsters. Apparently there was more than one of them, and they weren't monsters at all, but creatures called *humans*.

'We were going to tell you about humans after breakfast,' Min said. 'They can be a little ... overwhelming ... when you first see them, can't they?'

Hercufleas nodded.

'But the truth is, dear, they're not scary at all,' Min continued. 'All fleas – even big, talking fleas like us – are parasites. We can't live unless we have a host to live upon. Who do you think wears our house-hat?'

Hercufleas looked down at his feet. It felt strange to

think that the whole house was teetering on top of an enormous human head.

'We're not like normal fleas,' said Min. 'We're bigger. That means that we can't hide on our host, like other fleas. In fact, our host *invited* us to live in this hat.'

Hercufleas didn't understand. 'Why would he do that? Doesn't *The Plea of the Flea* say that humans call us pests and want to squish us?'

Min smiled. 'Our host is nice man called Mr Stickler, and he would never do that. We *work* for him, Hercufleas.'

'We do?'

She nodded. 'We're his employees. Or, in actual fact, his employ*fleas*. How else do you think we can afford blood from exotic animals all over the world, and to sleep on mouse-hair mattresses and light our rooms with candles? All these things cost money, and we have to work very hard to earn it. You too, eventually.'

Hercufleas slumped in his chair. What about the destiny he'd always known was waiting for him? What about adventures?

Something occurred to him. 'We won't *lose* our jobs, will we? Because of me biting our host, I mean? He won't think we're pests and make the fleamily leave his head?'

Min tried to smile, but she couldn't hide the worry in her voice. 'I hope not,' she said. 'It was just an accident, Hercufleas. A misunderstanding. But, you see . . .' She sighed. 'You didn't bite our host, you bit another human. A girl. One of Mr Stickler's *customers*. And this customer is very important to him. She has money, and she was about to pay him when you . . . well, when you made your mistake. Do you see now?'

Hercufleas nodded. Because of him, the girl might not feel like paying Mr Stickler, which meant he would lose business – and then the fleamily really *would* be pests to him.

'Will you come outside with me now and apologise?' Min asked.

Hercufleas was very nervous about seeing humans again. They were so big – so monstrously ugly. But Min needed him to say sorry, so he nodded. She leaned forward and nipped him on the cheek.

'What a sweet little hatchling you are. Come follow me, then. Don't be scared.'

Min led him out through the front door. They stood on the brim of the house-hat together. Despite all the koala blood, Hercufleas's legs were quivering. He suddenly realised he knew almost nothing about their host. He didn't even know what the customer wanted to buy.

So he asked Min, and just before they jumped onto Mr Stickler's shop counter, she whispered, 'He sells Happily Ever Afters.'

6

'You bring the quest, we'll do the rest' – that was the motto at Happily Ever Afters. Mr Stickler had it embroidered in gold thread across his blazer pocket. Standing nervously on the counter with Min and Pin, Hercufleas gazed up at him. Stickler wore a crisp suit the colour of banknotes. His wet eyes blinked, magnified behind scopical glasses. A thin black moustache squiggled across his lip like a signature on a contract. He had no visible neck; years of wearing the heavy house-hat had pushed it down into his shoulders.

So this is our host, thought Hercufleas, turning around. And this is his shop.

The walls of Happily Ever Afters were covered with posters advertising Avalonian heroes: paladins with swords, cossacks with bows, uhlans with long feathered lances. There were special offers like: 'Half price for quests involving beautiful princesses!' and 'Now with 33% more courage!'

'Mr Stickler rents heroes out to people who need a Happily Ever After,' Min explained in a whisper.

One day I'll be on that wall too, Hercufleas decided, imagining a poster with 'Whatever size his enemies, the winner's always Hercufleas!' written across it in bold.

'Well?' said Mr Stickler, glaring at Hercufleas. 'What do you say?'

'Oh!' Hercufleas was jolted from his daydream. He turned to the girl on the other side of the counter: the customer, who stood sucking her bleeding finger. 'Sorry for biting you.'

'Please forgive my little Hercufleas,' Min grovelled to the girl. 'He only hatched yesterday.'

'He's extremely adventurous,' Pin explained. 'We hope he'll grow out of it. The others did.'

'We've only ourselves to blame . . .' Min sighed. 'While in their eggs, they hear about nothing but heroes and quests and Happily Ever Afters, and then when they hatch—'

'He could have cost me a customer,' Stickler interrupted. 'Happily Ever Afters is a business. Our reputation is everything. We want to be known for helping people, not biting them.'

Hercufleas felt the drop of blood in his belly go hot with shame. 'But I thought—'

'I don't care what you thought,' Stickler snapped. 'I care what you did. You sullied our good name. What's to stop Miss Greta from going to another, rival shop to hire a hero?'

The customer took her finger from her mouth. 'He was trying to protect his family,' she said with a shrug. 'How can I be mad at someone who does that?'

'Miss Greta,' Stickler said, voice now wheedling, 'please accept again my sincere apologies for my employflea's temporary lapse in—'

'All right, all right, he's sorry, you're sorry, we're all sorry.' The girl called Greta rolled her eyes. 'Now how about you tell me what you can offer me? Then I can sign my contract, give you my gold, get my hero and go.'

Stickler blinked. 'As you wish.' He spread his hands wide. 'So, Miss Greta of Tumber, you want a hero. You've come to the right place. Avalon is famous for them. More live on this island than in the rest of the world put together. Here at Happily Ever Afters, we offer our customers only the finest heroes, the most legendary.'

'Well, where are they?' said Greta, looking around. 'I need one quick.'

Hercufleas waved his arm in the air. 'Ooh! Pick me!'

'Hush, little one!' Min clapped a hand over his mouth.

'Heroes are Avalon's most valuable resource,' Stickler explained. 'Gold must be kept safe in a vault, yes? Well, our heroes are no different. Here in Avalon they sleep in the caverns below our island until they are needed.'

Greta looked down at the floorboards. 'They're down there?'

'Deep down.'

'Asleep?'

'Indeed. Avalon's alchemists use potions to put them in an ageless slumber, while here at Happily Ever Afters, we painstakingly match each hero to the quest that best fits their capabilities. Then they are woken up to save the day, and later they are sent to sleep again. This method saves time, money and energy. It is an extremely efficient way to go on adventures.'

'How do we find the right hero for me, if they're all asleep?'

'Well, now . . .' Stickler flicked down a lens of his scopical glasses and peered closely at Greta. 'For that, we must look through the catalogues.'

7

Leaning below the counter, Mr Stickler cranked a hidden lever. Beneath Hercufleas, machinery began to rumble and whirr. A maze of dark cracks appeared across the countertop. With a clanking sound, high walls rose up on either side of him. Min held his hand tight and whispered, 'Don't worry, little one. Stay still and watch.'

With a hiss and shudder, the pistons and cogs below the counter groaned to a stop. Hercufleas looked around. The counter had transformed into a maze of corridors, with tall shelves either side stacked with books the size of stamps.

'These are my catalogues,' Stickler explained. 'A complete record of all the heroes I currently have available. Each book holds the details of one hero: their strengths, their weaknesses, their price . . .'

Greta gawped. 'That's the smallest library I've ever seen. Probably the biggest too. There must be thousands of books—'

'Seven thousand, nine hundred and fifty six,' said Min.

Greta looked at Stickler in awe. 'That's a lot of heroes.'

Stickler smirked. 'We have one for every conceivable purpose. Now tell me: what sort of hero do you need?'

She answered, 'A giant-slayer.'

Stickler nodded, glasses slipping down his shiny nose. 'Of course, of course, we have a fine selection, the finest in Avalon.' He peered down at Min, Pin and Hercufleas. 'You heard the customer. Find Miss Greta a giant-slayer.'

'At once, Mr Stickler!' Min and Pin grinned, relieved that they were still his employfleas.

'And keep your little hatchling under control.'

'We will, Mr Stickler!'

'And consider that a formal warning.'

'Certainly! Thank you, sir!'

Seizing hold of Hercufleas, his parents bounded down the corridors. The shelves flew past, all labelled with categories of heroes to suit any quest: Ninjas,

Nightmare-Hunters, Necromancers . . . So this was what Min meant when she said they worked for their host. His parents were the librarians of Stickler's catalogues of heroes.

'Tricky business, giant-slaying,' Stickler said above them, drumming his fingers on a shelf. 'Every giant has its weakness – an ogre is vulnerable to iron, a troll is susceptible to fire, and a cyclops is prone to conjunctivitis. Giants from the Cloud Kingdom, would you believe, are helpless against little boys called Jack—'

'Yuk doesn't come from the clouds,' Greta interrupted. 'He comes out of the forests around Tumber.'

'Hmm.' Stickler steepled his hands. 'Perhaps one of my stronger heroes will be able to simply overpower—'

'No,' Greta said. 'The mayor already tried that. He hired strong heroes from other shops: Heroes for Hire, and As Good As Our Sword, and BestQuest, I think, was the last one.'

'Hmm, BestQuest,' Stickler sniffed. 'Yes, they're just down the road. Although their heroes aren't quite as legendary as the ones we offer here, of course . . .'

'Good,' said Greta. 'Because we already hired the Stone Golem from there.'

'The Stone Golem? You hired him?' Stickler's voice was full of envy. 'He is the strongest hero BestQuest has to offer!'

'*Was* their strongest hero,' Greta corrected. 'He's a pile of gravel now.'

'Gravel?' Stickler choked on the word. 'Impossible.'

'I saw it happen,' said Greta. 'I was there.'

And while the fleas searched the miniature library below, Greta told Stickler about Yuk.

8

The night was dark, the moon was new and Yuk was coming. On the edge of Tumber, Greta snuffed her tinderlamp and hid behind some rubble to watch the approaching battle. She stared out into the blackness until she got her night vision. No light but the cold hard shining of the stars. Nothing stirring but the wind, rattling through the empty spaces between the pines. In that silence, her breath seemed too loud in her throat.

It started in the air. The air trembled. Again. Again. Like a heartbeat. Like a thunderstorm coming closer. Then the forest began to sway. Tall pines were parting like curtains. Two glowing moons the colour of curdled milk rose up into the sky from behind the tree line.

And *blinked*.

Yuk gazed down at Tumber. Each month he grew a

little bigger. With every guzzling he was a little stronger. Now he was at least ten houses high. The tree rooted on the top of his head stood up like a mohican. The bats roosting in the cavern of his bellybutton uttered their eerie screams. Shaggy moss covered his body and a tangled beard of vines trailed down his chest. His mouth was full of grey broken teeth, covered with lichen like tombstones. He ground them together, then roared:

'YUK WANTS TO GUZZLE!'

In one stride he reached the river; in another he crossed it. Greta watched him stomp down the dead streets, plunging his hand into houses with roofs already torn off like the tops of sardine tins. Yuk had guzzled them, months ago.

'WHERE'S YUK'S FOOD?' he bellowed.

Enraged, his fists smashed the houses to bits. Bricks and bits of chimney sploshed in the river. When the echoes of his voice faded away, Yuk turned to look up at the Church of Saint Katerina on the Hill, where the last tinderlamps were still lit. Licking his lips, he stepped forward.

Right into the ambush.

'I shall protect Tumber!' boomed a voice, and down the hill charged the Stone Golem of Prais.

The Stone Golem, chiselled from granite and brought to life by alchemy!

The Stone Golem, said to be indestructible!

The Stone Golem, who had once punched the ground so hard with his fist, the Earth wobbled out of orbit and descended into a winter ten years long!

His charge took Yuk by surprise. He smashed into the giant's shin, sending Yuk stumbling back down the hill. But the giant was back on his feet at once, towering over the mighty hero.

The Stone Golem attacked again, but this time Yuk was ready. Raising one enormous foot, he stamped on the hero, grinding him beneath his heel. The Stone Golem's granite body began to crack and splinter under the pressure. Yuk jumped up and down, pulverising the hero again – again – again – until there was nothing left but gravel.

Licking his lips, the giant reached the Church of Saint Katerina on the Hill. He tore off the roof and plunged in his hand . . .

'Enough!' shrieked Stickler. 'I've heard all I need to hear!'

Greta fell silent. In the library stacks, Hercufleas tried in vain to imagine Yuk's size. To him, humans were enormous. But Yuk . . . the giant's *blood cells* were probably bigger than he was. What hero could possibly stop something so gargantuan?

'Gnome-catchers, goblin-trappers . . .' Behind him, Min and Pin hopped along the shelves, reading labels.

'Here we are: giant-slayers.'

But just as they reached the first book, the shelves sank back down again with a shudder. Gears whining, they juddered back below the counter and vanished.

'Apologies,' Stickler said to Greta, taking his hand from the lever. 'We are currently experiencing technical issues. I'm afraid it won't be possible to help you. Goodbye, and have a Happily Ever After.'

9

Hercufleas looked at Min and Pin. They stared back, as confused as he was. Above them, Mr Stickler sat, hands folded, waiting for Greta to leave the shop.

She did not.

'What do you mean, you won't help me?' She scowled. 'Why?'

'At current, we currently have no suitable heroes, erm, currently available.' Stickler blinked nervously.

'You didn't even look!' Greta cried. 'You're afraid!'

'Afraid?' Stickler barked a laugh. 'Ridiculous.'

'You are. You're terrified of Yuk!'

'He could damage my top earners!' Stickler said primly. 'Your quest sounds as if it has already wasted a good number of heroes. I recommend you try BestQuest again, or As Good As Our Sword.'

'Or me!' Hercufleas piped up.

'Hercufleas, hush!' said Min.

'Goodbye,' said Stickler. 'The door is located behind you. Use it at your earliest convenience.'

Greta locked her eyes on him. 'You'll help me,' she growled, 'or else.'

He snorted. 'Or else what?'

Her eyes brimmed. 'Or else *this*,' she said, bottom lip quivering.

Stickler folded his arms. 'Crying won't get you anywhere.'

'He wouldn't help me,' Greta sniffed, looking around the shop as if people were there. 'Mr Stickler, from Happily Ever Afters. I only wanted a hero, and he sent away a poor helpless child in need!'

Stickler looked around in confusion. 'Who are you . . .? What are you . . . ?' But Greta drowned him out with an anguished howl and burst into tears. They dribbled down her cheeks and hung from her chin in wobbly drops.

'Why wouldn't he help?' she sobbed to the invisible crowd. 'Happily Ever Afters had such a good reputation! "You bring the quest, we'll do the rest," he says, but that's not truuuuue.'

Mr Stickler reared back in alarm. 'Stop it! Don't . . .

You mustn't say that to anyone!'

'I can't help it,' Greta wailed, heading for the door. 'I'm just so saaaaaad! I'm never going to stop being saaaad, or telling everyone just who made me saaaad!'

'Hold it!' Stickler said in a panic. 'Be quiet! Shut up!'

Greta only cried harder, louder. She opened the shop door to the street.

'All right!' Stickler lunged forward, catching hold of her satchel and yanking her back inside. 'It's all right, you can stop crying, you can shut the door! I remember now!'

Her tears stopped at once. Greta turned to him, eyes red and triumphant. 'Remember what?'

'I know who can give you your Happily Ever After.' Stickler sank back into his chair, dabbing his sweaty forehead with his sleeve.

Greta sniffed. 'Who?'

'Me?' suggested Hercufleas.

'They are the greatest warriors in all Avalon,' Stickler said quickly. 'Happily Ever Afters only offers them, you understand, for the riskiest, most perilous of quests . . . I do not think they have been awoken in decades.'

Greta came back to the counter. 'What are their names?' she said eagerly.

'Prince Xin,' said Mr Stickler. 'And Ugor the Barbarian.'

'Prince Who?' said Min.

'Ugor the What?' said Pin.

'Never heard of them,' they said together.

Hercufleas frowned. Mr Stickler was hiding something he was ashamed of . . . maybe even afraid of, too. Being a flea, to whom keeping out of sight was second nature, Hercufleas could sense it. But what could it be? He looked at Min, but she just shrugged.

'We've never hired them out before,' she murmured.

Greta narrowed her eyes at Mr Stickler, obviously suspicious too. He avoided her gaze and took off his glasses to polish them.

'Are you trying to swindle me?'

'Swindle you? No, no! Of course not! I give you my one-hundred-per-cent money-back guarantee.'

Hercufleas believed him. If Mr Stickler *was* trying to swindle Greta, surely that would ruin his reputation just as much as if he'd refused to help her. But what was he up to, then? Hercufleas couldn't work it out.

Neither could Greta. She scrutinised Mr Stickler, then rolled her eyes and gave up. 'Have Prince Xin and Ugor got experience slaying giants? I don't need them strong, I don't need them to have enchanted swords, I just need *giant-slayers.* Understand?'

'Oh yes!' Stickler nodded furiously, the house-hat wobbling on his head. 'Of course. Now, there are certain . . . risks . . . attached to Prince Xin and Ugor . . . And the fee to hire such legendary warriors is, of course, considerable . . .'

Greta leaned down and fiddled with a clog. Three enormous gold coins flicked up into the air. Hercufleas leaped clear as they clattered onto the counter.

Stickler leaned forward to gaze at the florins. Their reflections glittered in his scopical glasses. The muscles in his jaw twitched. 'That should be . . . more than sufficient,' he said. 'Now all you have to do to seal the deal is sign the contract. Where are the rest of my employfleas?'

'Here, Mr Stickler!' The rest of the fleamily exploded out of the house-hat like miniature cannonballs, from the door and the windows and even the chimney. They landed in a drawer that Stickler pulled open. First they lugged an enormous blank sheet of paper out onto the counter. Next they rolled a black bottle of ink out beside it. Finally they gathered pairs of strange iron boots, which they tied tightly to their feet. Hercufleas looked on in bewilderment.

'Pin and I are Mr Stickler's librarians,' Min explained, seeing his confusion. 'The rest of you have a different job.'

'Wear these,' Itch called to him, tossing Hercufleas two iron shoes. 'You can be X and Q today – they're the easiest.'

Hercufleas looked at the large letters stamped on the soles. He slipped the shoes on and hopped over to the inkpot, where his brothers and sisters sat on the rim, dipping their feet into the black liquid.

'Don't worry.' Burp grinned. 'Just watch and learn.'

He held up his feet for Hercufleas to see. He had the letters A and S. Looking around, Hercufleas saw they had almost the whole alphabet between them.

With a small jump, he realised that his brothers and sisters were Mr Stickler's typewriter.

Stickler turned to the fleamily and spoke to them in what sounded to Hercufleas like a foreign language. He heard the phrases *P23 hero-hire contract, money-back-guarantee coupon* and *discretionary peril insurance form.* He had no idea what any of it meant, but everyone else seemed to understand completely.

'Ready?' yelled Speck, over by the blank piece of paper.

'Steady?' yelled Fleck.

'Type!' they all cried together.

10

The fleamily leaped onto the pristine page, bouncing back and forth. Their shoes left letters wherever they landed, like footprints. Burp somersaulted over Dot, Tittle bounded over Jot, Speck and Fleck added commas and full stops.

In a few minutes, Greta's contract was almost ready. The fleamily pulled Hercufleas from the inkpot and showed him the one or two blank spaces on the paper that he had to fill in with his own letters. He jumped clumsily from spot to spot, while Titch yelled out, 'Left foot!' or 'Right foot!' so he knew which letter to land with.

'Don't worry!' Slurp called as Hercufleas typed a Q upside down by mistake. 'We can practise in the boingy-boing room! It's fun when you get the hang of it.'

But Slurp was wrong. It wasn't fun; it would never be fun; it was awful. Hercufleas felt like crying, which is a terrible feeling for fleas especially, because they have no tear ducts.

Inside his egg, life had seemed so simple: hatch, become a hero, go on adventures. But that was impossible now. He didn't get to go on the quests; he just typed up the forms.

'What's wrong, Hercufleas?' Min said. She smiled. 'Wait, don't tell me. I know.'

'You do?'

'You're *hungry*, aren't you?' She shook her head. 'You hatchlings and your appetites!'

Hercufleas nodded. But he was hungry for adventures, not for blood.

'Just add in a Q there, and an X there, then you're finished.' Min pointed at the contract's final few blank spaces. Over by the inkpot, the fleas were slinging off their typing shoes and hopping up Stickler's sleeve towards the house-hat. 'Follow us up to the house-hat and I'll mix you up a nice cocktail: bee, bear and butterfly blood. It buzzes in your mouth, growls down your throat and flutters in your belly. That'll cheer you up!' She nipped him on the cheek and bounded off.

Hercufleas sighed. A blood cocktail might make him feel better, for a little bit. But then tomorrow would come, with more customers, more contracts, more typing . . .

Stickler whipped the contract like a rug from beneath his feet, sending him sprawling.

'That'll do,' Stickler said, plucking a quill from his pocket. 'Here's your peril insurance form, Miss Greta . . . Here's your money-back-guarantee coupon . . . And to receive your heroes, sign on the dotted lines: here, here and here.'

Greta snatched the quill and stabbed it down into the inkpot, scratching her name several times across the paper. Stickler blew the ink dry, then filed the contract away in a drawer.

'You've got your gold and your signature,' she said, looking around. 'Now where are my heroes?'

Hercufleas felt something buzz inside him, as if he had drunk the blood of an electric eel. Were Prince Xin and Ugor the Barbarian really coming here? Was he about to glimpse the most legendary heroes in all Avalon? Shivers ran up and down his spine.

'I will send a message to our alchemists to wake them and dispatch them from the caverns below,' Stickler explained. 'Prince Xin and Ugor will meet you by the shore.'

Hercufleas's excitement fizzed away. Not only was he not going on any adventures, he wasn't even going to see the heroes that were. It wasn't fair!

'How will I find them?' Greta pointed out the window. 'It's dark. And there's fog.'

Stickler scooped up the florins. 'Don't worry about finding them – they'll find you. They will be looking.' He held out a slip of paper for Greta to take. 'Show them your receipt, and have a Happily Ever After.'

Hercufleas looked around. His fleamily were already back in the house-hat. He saw their silhouettes through the kitchen window. Stickler's attention was focused completely on the gold florins in his hands. Greta was stuffing the receipt into her satchel.

No one was watching him.

His legs jumped before his brain could tell him what a stupid idea it was. He landed on the back of Greta's collar and crouched there, utterly still, as she headed for the door. He heard the shop bell ring as she walked outside. He saw the goosebumps on her neck rise in the cold night mist.

What am I doing? he wondered. But his heart knew the answer. It thrummed in his chest with a giddy thrill. He was going on an adventure!

Only a little one, of course. Ten minutes at most. He deserved it, after all that hard work. He was going to catch a glimpse of Prince Xin and Ugor the Barbarian, the greatest heroes in all Avalon. Then he'd hop back to Happily Ever Afters. With a bit of luck, no one would even notice he was gone.

11

Greta ran through dark, foggy streets, heading for the shore. The air was thick and chill and dank. Tucked under her collar, Hercufleas shivered. Glimpses of Avalon emerged from the mist and vanished again just as quickly. Rows of sulphur-yellow street lamps. Posters in shop windows advertising heroes for hire. Statues of legendary knights, hair and shoulders crusty with gull poo and rime. Street sellers hawking merchandise, holding out to Greta replicas of famous swords, alchemicals granting super-strength and matryoshka dolls from Petrossia.

The outside world astounded Hercufleas. He hadn't realised just how enormous Avalon would be. It was going to take him forever to hop back to Happily Ever Afters and the house-hat. He pushed the thought from his mind. Adventurers didn't worry about getting home.

They kept going no matter what.

Greta kept going too, clogs clack-clack-clacking on the cobbles, until she reached the pebbly shore. She skidded to a stop, panting for breath, heart racing. Hercufleas's heart, the size of an apple pip, beat just as hard. This was where Stickler had told Greta to wait. This was where the heroes were supposed to be.

'Prince Xin?' called Greta into the mist. 'Ugor? Hello?'

Hercufleas strained his ears for a reply, but there was only the lap of the waves on the shore and the faraway thud of Greta's enormous heart. Wait. Now he heard something else – the scrunch of shingle. Footsteps.

Coming closer.

Slowly Hercufleas edged from Greta's collar to her shoulder. He couldn't come all this way (and get in what would probably be an enormous amount of trouble) without seeing the heroes. Two enormous silhouettes stood up ahead, the mist curling its white fingers around them. Prince Xin and Ugor the Barbarian. Real heroes. Hercufleas clapped his hands over his mouth to stop himself screaming with excitement.

'You are Greta?' said Prince Xin, moving forward. He was slender as a willow cane, with skin flawless as porcelain and eyes the colour of jade.

'I am.' Greta waved her receipt. 'I've hired you for a deadly quest.'

Prince Xin's laugh was sensuous and dreamy, like a love song. 'Have you now?' He reached down and stroked the feathers of the enormous creature he sat astride. It was the size of a horse. It had stunted wings, the legs of an ostrich and the neck and plumage of a swan. 'Did you hear that, Artifax? Doesn't sound very appealing, does it?'

Artifax cocked his eagle head and clucked softly, regarding Greta with his purple eyes.

'Hundreds of lives are at stake,' Greta persisted, stepping closer. 'We must go at once.'

'Ugor and Onk-Onk not care about hundreds of lives, just our own,' the barbarian said, emerging from the mist. He was twice as tall as the prince, and twelve times as broad, and a thousand times as hairy. Hercufleas wrinkled his nose: Ugor smelled of gunpowder and swill. He sat atop a huge armoured pig that could fire bullets from its snout.

'But you *have* to help!' said Greta, confusion and panic in her voice. 'You cost all the gold I had.' She waved the receipt at them again. 'You're the greatest heroes in all Avalon!'

'Is that what Stickler told you?' Prince Xin rolled

his eyes. 'That man is so devious he almost puts *me* to shame!'

Ugor the Barbarian laughed. It sounded like dynamite rumbling up a mineshaft. Hercufleas saw his teeth were filed down to sharp points, and suddenly he was afraid.

Greta scowled. 'Why are you laughing?'

Prince Xin's smile slid from his face. His laugh was different now. Sharp and hard. 'Do we look like heroes to you?'

Hercufleas watched them uneasily, his insides wriggling and twisting, as if he'd drunk worm blood. What did Prince Xin mean? Why had he drawn his sword? What was Ugor doing, stuffing bullets down Onk-Onk's snout?

Were they . . . ?

Did they mean . . . ?

Surely they couldn't be . . .

Hercufleas felt Greta tremble. He watched the hairs on the back of her neck prickle and rise. He began to whisper *The Plea of the Flea* under his breath.

Greta backed away. 'You're scaring me.'

'Of course we're scaring you.' Prince Xin sighed theatrically. 'Isn't that what villains are supposed to do?'

Greta went pale as the mist. 'Villains? But I need a

Happily Ever After—'

'Did you think only *good* people want Happily Ever Afters?' said Prince Xin. 'There are plenty of ambitious princes who want their fathers to vacate the throne. Wicked alchemists needing children to practise their potions upon. People like that don't need a hero to do good – they need a villain to do evil. That's why Mr Stickler keeps us. We make him a fortune.' He frowned. 'But you know all this, surely. Unless Stickler gave us to you by mistake.'

'No, he picked you out for me especially, after I threatened to—' Greta began, and then stopped. Suddenly it all fell into place. Prince Xin and Ugor weren't going to help Greta take care of Yuk, they were going to help Mr Stickler take care of Greta . . .

'Ah,' said Prince Xin softly. 'Now I understand. You threatened Mr Stickler? He doesn't like that. He's very proud of his reputation. He'll do dreadful things to protect it. Or, rather, he'll get us to do the dreadful things for him.'

'Oh run, Greta,' Hercufleas urged, his voice growing from a whisper to a shout. 'Run, run, run, you have to RUN!'

12

Greta whirled round and pelted away from the villains, tripping and skidding across the shingle. A panic-stricken Hercufleas held on to her collar as she ran.

There was a whistling sound, something fluttered through the mist overhead and Prince Xin floated down in front of her, light as a feather, blocking her escape. It wasn't a sword in his hand, Hercufleas realised, but a silver fluted tube – a flyte. Flytes were rare instruments that he'd heard his fleamily talk about. They gave heroes skilled enough to play them the power to glide through the air like a bird.

'It really is nothing personal,' said Prince Xin. 'A job is a job, and we pride ourselves on always completing our contract.'

'Get away from me!' Greta yelled, reaching for the axe

slung across her back. 'Help! Somebody help me!'

She aimed a chop at Prince Xin, who piped a melody and soared up out of reach. Behind Greta, Ugor nudged Onk-Onk left and right, aiming the barrels of his snout.

'Behind you!' Hercufleas yelled in Greta's ear.

There was a loud booming roar, a flash of powder. He heard the bullets zip over him as Greta ducked. She rolled left, and Prince Xin trilled a frantic high note to get out of the way, just in time – he glared down at the two smouldering holes in the end of his blue cloak.

'That was midnight velvet!' Prince Xin snarled, perfect face twisted with rage. Because he stopped playing the flyte to speak, he dropped to the ground. Greta swung her axe again, but he caught the handle and wrenched it from her grasp.

'Now you will see why they call Ugor the Ballistic Barbarian,' Ugor grinned, reaching for his gun on Onk-Onk's saddle.

'No, no, no!' said Prince Xin crossly. 'Don't *shoot* her! Then it will be obvious she has been murdered. Stickler won't want the rest of Avalon to find out about this! No, I have a *much* better idea. Watch!'

He sprang forward, dodging Greta's wild punches. He

snatched her up, kicking and screaming, with one hand. With the other he began to play his flyte.

They rose up into the fog. Hercufleas's stomach lurched. Higher, higher, higher they went, until the ground below disappeared and there was nothing but whiteness all around. Then they burst out above the mist. The cold stars shone like blue diamonds beside a sliver of moon.

Far below, Ugor was shouting. 'Where you go, Xin? What you do?'

Hercufleas knew. Once he got high enough, Prince Xin would simply let Greta go. All they had to do was lay her body at the bottom of the island's cliffs. It would look as if she had lost her footing in the mist. A tragic accident.

Beautiful, haunting music came from the flyte. The arpeggios rose, higher and higher. Any moment, they would reach a crescendo, and Greta would drop like a stone. She twisted and screamed, trying to get free, but Prince Xin was too strong, and gradually the fight ebbed from her.

With a desperate scream, Hercufleas launched himself from her shoulder.

'Whatever size his enemies, the winner's always HERCUFLEAS!' he bellowed.

And landing on the flyte, he bit Prince Xin's fingers as hard as he possibly could.

'OWWW!'

At once the haunting music stopped and they were all tumbling down, head over heels through the air. Hercufleas clung to the flyte for dear life. Prince Xin snatched for the instrument, but Hercufleas gnashed at his fingers again and he jerked his hand away with a howl. Greta lunged for the flyte, brought it to her lips and managed to blow a single high note that pinned her in place in the air.

Prince Xin grabbed at her feet. He pulled off a clog and disappeared with a hideous shriek down into the fog.

Three seconds later, the shriek ended in a sickening thud on the shingle below.

Down on the ground, Ugor roared.

Hercufleas opened his eyes. His arms and legs were wrapped around the end of the flyte. Prince Xin's sickly-sweet blood was still in his mouth, tasting of jasmine and malice. Shakily he pulled himself up and stood on the tip of the instrument. Greta was still playing the high note, like the wail of a boiling kettle, keeping them suspended in the air. Her eyes were wide. Her pupils were almost crossed, staring at Hercufleas on the end of the flyte.

'Whatever you do,' he shouted, 'don't stop playing.'

Greta nodded, but now the high note was beginning to wobble. She was running out of breath.

She gasped a lungful of air, but as the note ended, the flyte's magic ceased. They plunged down. Greta sank into the mist up to her knees, then blew the same note and jerked to a stop again.

'Can you play something higher?' Hercufleas yelled. 'To take us up?'

Greta screwed her eyes shut, she shook with effort until she was beetroot red, but no matter how hard she blew, she didn't have the breath or skill to make the flyte take them higher.

69

They fell further down into the mist as she took another breath.

And again: lower.

Lower.

'You coming back down to me, little Greta,' said Ugor from below. His voice was much closer now. 'Ugor waiting for you. You die for poor Prince Xin.'

Now they were level with the street lamps lining the shore. The ground was a brown haze beneath them. Hercufleas made out Ugor's enormous dark shape. He heard Artifax clucking softly over the body of Prince Xin.

They only had a few seconds before they hit the ground. Hercufleas scrabbled about in his mind, trying to cobble together a plan. Greta looked at him desperately. She couldn't speak, but he knew what she was asking. She was begging him to save her. To be her hero.

'Stay as high as you can, for as long as you can,' he said. 'I'll get help.'

Greta shook her head. *Don't leave me.*

'I have to,' he said. 'I can't fight Ugor. He's like a giant compared to me.'

Tears leaked from her screwed-up eyes.

'I'll get help,' he said. 'Stay here. Don't —'

And then Greta ran out of breath again, and they fell.

13

Ugor snatched Greta by her brambly hair. She kicked and flailed, trying to put the flyte to her lips again. He tore it from her grasp and crushed it to bits. Hercufleas tumbled off the end of the instrument, an invisible dot in the night. He landed headfirst in Onk-Onk's left nostril. The pig sniffed, and with a yell Hercufleas was sucked up its snout.

There, at the end of a long tunnel packed with gunpowder and bogeys, he had an idea.

Before his brain could tell him what a stupid, reckless and dangerously explosive idea it was, Hercufleas rolled himself into a ball, shut his eyes and bit down as hard as he could.

Onk-Onk sneezed.

With a bright blue flash, a gigantic force shoved

Hercufleas in the back. He shot out of Onk-Onk's snout at well over a thousand miles an hour.

Straight into Ugor!

There was a *clang!* like a blacksmith's anvil. The barbarian stumbled backwards, his armoured breastplate dented and cracked. Hercufleas felt as if he'd been hit with a sledgehammer. He fell on the ground, winded and dazed.

Above him, Greta stood blinking in confusion, wondering how she was still alive. Then she spotted a little brown pebble on the beach stagger to its feet.

Her hero.

'Urggh . . .' said Ugor. 'Bad Onk-Onk . . . Why you break Ugor's best armour?'

Greta had a fraction of a second to escape. She grabbed Hercufleas with one hand and her axe in the other, and ran. Ugor staggered to his feet in a daze.

'Back to the house-hat!' gasped Hercufleas in her palm. He lay there thinking of his fleamily and how he would never, ever go adventuring again.

But Greta ran to the shore, where a beautiful white bird stood over the body of Prince Xin. Behind her, Ugor jumped on Onk-Onk, who squealed as he charged towards them.

'Stop!' urged Hercufleas. 'You're going the wrong way!'

In one leap, Greta was on Artifax's back, nestling between his little wings.

'Go!' she said. 'Go!'

Artifax twisted his long neck round to stare at her, head cocked.

'GO, Artifax!'

Then the bird saw Onk-Onk rushing up from behind, and suddenly they shot forward like an arrow from a bow. Down the shingle they flew, towards the waves. Ugor roared and cursed but Artifax outran his shouts. In a matter of seconds he had reached a jetty. He ran on, right to the very end, right to where there was no more jetty, only waves.

They didn't stop.

Or sink.

Faster than the wind, Artifax splashed across the water like a skipped stone. When Hercufleas looked back towards Avalon, the lights of the island had already vanished into the mist.

It was pitch dark upon the lake. The only sounds were the *splish-splish-splish* of Artifax's feet and the howl of the wind through his feathers. And at that moment it struck

Hercufleas – with as much force as he had struck Ugor – that nothing would be the same again.

The house-hat, the exotic blood, the boingy-boing room – all of it would have to end. Mr Stickler hired out villains. He was not an agent just of good, but of evil. And because he was their host, without knowing it the fleamily lived off evil too.

Now Hercufleas knew the truth, they'd have to leave. They would become just like other fleas, scavenging blood wherever they could, always at risk of being squished by thumbs or drowned in hot soapy baths.

His adventure had ruined everything. But if he hadn't left with Greta, *she* would be the dead one now, instead of Prince Xin. Hercufleas might have saved her life . . . but the life his fleamily had known? The life Hercufleas had lived for one, wonderful day?

That was over.

14

With a cluck, Artifax emerged from the mist and stepped back onto dry land, feet thudding on soft sand. They had crossed the lake to the far shore. Avalon was behind them. Up ahead were endless hills and forests.

The kingdom of Petrossia.

Artifax slowed to a stop, his sides heaving, and began preening his feathers. Hercufleas lay in Greta's hand, miserable.

In the dark stillness, she leaned into her palm, so close that he felt the warm wind of her breath.

'Are you alive?'

'Unfortunately, yes,' said Hercufleas. 'I'm sorry.'

'Sorry? What for?'

'It was only supposed to be a little adventure, I promise . . . But it ended up a huge disaster, didn't it?

Now you won't get your Happily Ever After, and my fleamily will be homeless, and I never, ever should have left the house-hat . . .'

He trailed off. Greta's eyes shone. Her shoulders shook. She was giggling.

'What's so funny?'

She threw back her head and howled with laughter so hard she fell off Artifax and onto the sand.

'Oh, Hercufleas!' she cried, tears streaming from her odd-coloured eyes. 'You're not a disaster, you're incredible! You're unbe*flea*vable! You're *parasitic*ulous! The *best pest* in all the world! You're perfect! What a hero I'm bringing back to Tumber!'

Hercufleas hopped to his feet. 'Did you just call me a hero?'

Greta grinned, jumping up and dancing around Artifax, who cocked his head and squawked. 'Not just a hero, but exactly the right type of hero too.'

Hercufleas gawped. 'I am?'

'Of course!' laughed Greta. 'You're a *giant-slayer!* You saved me from Prince Xin, *and* from Ugor. Compared to you, those two are *colossal*!'

And she gave him an enormous slobbery kiss.

'Eurgh!' he spluttered. 'Yuck!'

Greta froze. 'Yuk!' she cried. 'Of course! We have to get you to Tumber, so you can fight Yuk! Don't worry, you won't have to do it on your own – you can teach the Tumberfolk about giant-slaying, and they'll help!'

Hercufleas blinked. What could he teach the Tumberfolk? All he'd done was bite someone's finger, then hide in a pig's nostril and cause a small explosion. And yet the thought made him puff with pride. He was a giant-slayer! A heroic giant-slayer!

'We've got to leave right now,' Greta said. 'We'll have to go through the forests – my boat is back in Avalon. And so is my other clog. But we've got Artifax.' She looked at the great bird's tiny wings and sighed. 'I wish Prince Xin had bred your wings a bit bigger – then we could fly over the trees instead of stumbling through them.' She turned to Hercufleas. 'No time to lose! Are you ready?'

It was all happening so fast. Greta was asking him to join her on another adventure. She wanted him to save her again. His destiny was unfolding, right in front of him. So why was he hesitating?

'Shouldn't we go back to Avalon first?' he said. 'We have to explain what happened, or—'

Greta scowled. 'You saw what Ugor tried to do. He'll be watching. If I so much as set foot on that island . . .

And then there's Stickler . . .' Her face went dark with rage. 'He tried to have me killed.'

'Maybe he made a mistake, maybe it was an administrative error . . .' Hercufleas trailed off. He knew Greta was right. Stickler was just as villainous as Prince Xin and Ugor. He only cared about his business, his reputation and his gold. Greta knew his dark secret, and if they returned to Avalon, Stickler would try to get rid of her. And maybe Hercufleas too.

'This isn't about Stickler any more,' Greta said, pulling him from his thoughts. 'This is about Tumber.' She pointed up at the last sliver of moon. 'Tomorrow, when the moon is new, Yuk will come to guzzle everyone I've ever known. Won't you help?'

Hercufleas hopped back and forth across her palm, trying to make the right choice. He could return to Avalon and bring Stickler to justice, or go to Tumber and rescue the people there from Yuk.

'I'll come with you, Greta,' he said at last. 'But first I have to go back to Happily Ever Afters.'

She stared at him. 'But—'

'I have to warn my fleamily,' said Hercufleas firmly. 'They might be in danger. What if Stickler tries to hurt them too?'

'But—'

'I'm small. I can sneak back to Avalon without being spotted. I'll go straight to the owners of BestQuest, or Heroes for Hire, and tell them the truth.

'But—'

'Stop saying "but"! I have to do this. I don't have a choice.'

Greta scowled. 'Neither do I.'

Her hand closed into a fist, squeezing him like the coils of a python.

'Greta! What are you doing? Let me go!'

He bit and kicked and tried to jump, but she only tightened her grip.

'Ride, Artifax!' she called, leaping onto the bird's back. They hurtled forward into the trees and entered the land of Petrossia.

15

On they rode through the forest. It was just like an adventure in an Avalonian fairy tale: a brave hero, a noble steed, a fair maiden. Except the brave hero was the size of a raisin, the fair maiden was a scowling kidnapper and the noble steed was some sort of gigantic albino chicken.

It was not an adventure Hercufleas wanted to be a part of.

He had fought in Greta's grip, biting and struggling and yelling until he was exhausted. Eventually his rage cooled to a dull anger and his anger froze into icy terror. There was nothing he could do. Greta was taking him off to fight a giant that had crushed Avalon's strongest hero into little pieces.

What terrified Hercufleas even more than Yuk was

what might be happening to his fleamily right now. They had no idea that their host was a greedy attempted-murderer who hired out villains as well as heroes.

He imagined Stickler taking his hat from his head and shaking it up and down on the porch, yelling, 'I told you to keep your little hatchling under control! I gave you a formal warning!' He imagined Min, Pin and the others huddling together in the mist, shivering, hungry, homeless. He imagined Stickler deciding the fleamily needed to be silenced to protect his reputation . . .

He had to make Greta let him go. Whatever it took.

He started off with lies.

'Greta, I think I've sprained my ankle.'

'Greta, I've just remembered – I left my sword back in Avalon!'

'Greta, I'm allergic to giants. They give me a rash.'

When lies didn't work, he tried threats.

'Greta, you have until the count of three to let me out, otherwise I'll bite you, suck out all your blood and leave you here like a shrivelled-up prune! One . . . Two . . . Two and a half . . . Two and almost very nearly three . . .'

He tried curses. ('I hope Yuk eats you right after he eats me!') He tried begging. ('Please, please, please, please, *please* let me go.') Nothing worked.

After hours of stumbling between trees, Hercufleas felt Greta's fingers start to loosen their grip, until finally she let him go completely.

'I'm sorry,' she said curtly. 'I shouldn't have snatched you like that. Come on, you can hop on my shoulder if you want.'

Hercufleas ignored her. He stood in her palm, stretching his stiff legs. Now it was his turn to scowl. 'What makes you think I'm coming with you?' he said.

'I'm hopping back to Avalon to save my fleamily—'

'Your fleamily will be fine,' Greta interrupted. 'For now. We can deal with Stickler later.'

'What if he gets rid of them, like he tried to get rid of you?'

'Why would he? He needs them. They're his employfleas.'

'But if he thinks that I . . .' Hercufleas couldn't bring himself to say *murdered*. 'If he realises that Prince Xin . . . If he finds out that was *me*—'

'He won't. Think about it. Ugor didn't even *see* you. And you didn't tell anyone where you were going, did you?'

Hercufleas shook his head. Greta had a point. 'But it still feels wrong to leave them,' he said.

Greta gave a huff and plonked him on Artifax's head. Then she slid onto the ground, plucked some brambleberries from a bush and fed them to the bird, one by one.

'Also,' she added quietly while Artifax pecked, 'if you *did* try and escape, I doubt you'd make it very far. You might be a good giant-slayer, but that won't help you in here.'

Hercufleas looked around. Trees in every direction. The whole place silent and somehow lifeless . . . He shook his jitters away. What was there to be scared of? It was just a wood.

Greta seemed to sense his thoughts. 'We're not in Avalon any more. This is Petrossia, and Petrossia doesn't have woods. It has *woodn'ts* instead.'

Artifax finished his meal, clucking with pleasure, and Greta stroked his neck before whispering, 'Know how the woodn't got its name, Hercufleas? Because you *wouldn't* want to go through it. Not if you had a choice.'

Hercufleas sighed. He didn't believe her. She was just trying to make him stay. 'What should I be scared of then?' he asked. 'Is the Bögenmann coming to get us?'

Greta shook her head. 'No, the Bögenmann lives miles away to the west,' she said. 'Here it's mainly wolves and black bears and grizzly squirrels.'

Hercufleas chuckled. 'Grizzly squirrels?'

'Give me a wolf or a black bear over a grizzly squirrel any day,' she said. 'At least they can't climb trees. Although you shouldn't ever climb trees in a woodn't. They're the most dangerous things of all.'

Greta's words made Hercufleas's insides cold and squirmy, as if he'd drunk slug blood. 'Trees? What's dangerous about trees?'

'Nothing.' Greta shrugged. 'Unless you're in a woodn't. Here, they're big. And hungry.'

Hercufleas shivered.

Trees?

Hungry?

'The woodn't is so thick,' Greta said, 'sunlight gets blotted out before it reaches the floor. The trees that grow beneath the canopy have to find something other than sunbeams to feed on. Pine-needlers feed on birds. Bramble-strangle feeds on other trees. Rattlesnoaks are the worst. They camouflage themselves to look just like normal oaks, but their roots move, and each rattleroot has a snake's head at the end. A bite from one of them will paralyse you in seconds. Then they drag you towards the trunk, and the rattlesnoak gobbles you up.'

A branch creaked behind Hercufleas. He jumped up, hitting his head on a leaf, which made him scream, which made Greta laugh.

'It's autumn now,' she said. 'So all the rattleroots will be settling down to hibernate. And right now they have seed pods on their branches that shake when anyone gets too close. Over there: listen . . .'

Hercufleas strained his ears. Far to his left, above the rustle of the woodn't, he heard a harsh rattling, like a dozen maracas shaking, and then, far off, a wolf's howl. He trembled. Beneath his feet, so did Artifax.

'You know a lot about this woodn't, Greta.'

'I have to. I'm a woodcutter.' She tapped the axe on her back and smiled sadly. 'Just like my parents were.'

In the distance, the rattlesnoak shook again, and Greta's eyes got a faraway look in them.

'Once,' she told him, 'before the guzzlings, Papa crept up on a rattlesnoak and carved Mama's name into its trunk.

Then he chopped off one of its roots, to prove he'd done it, and made her this axe.'

She showed Hercufleas the gnarled handle of her axe, which ended in the varnished head of a snake. It looked as if it was carved into the wood, but Hercufleas knew now that it wasn't.

A tree, with serpent roots.

'Mama always used to tell me that story.' Greta fell quiet. 'Are you hungry?'

Hercufleas realised suddenly that yes, he was. Hungry and scared.

'Lion blood, if you have any?' he said, then seeing her glare, added, 'Cougar or panther blood will do.'

Greta held out her thumb. 'Drink,' she said.

Hercufleas winced at the memory of Greta's bitter-tasting blood. He'd prefer to drink from Artifax, but that might be rude. So he nipped her and took a quick sip. Just like last time, it puckered his mouth and made him shudder as it slid down his throat – but then the aftertaste carried a hint of something sweet that hadn't been there before. It was hope. Greta believed in Hercufleas. She truly thought he was the one to save her town. Now there was no longer only bitterness inside her.

★

The woodn't grew lighter, and suddenly they found themselves in a clearing where all the trees were overturned or jagged stumps. In the starlight, the valley was a colour both black and emerald. The moon was a white sliver.

'Did . . . Did Yuk do this?' Hercufleas looked out across the jumble of broken trees and churned earth.

Greta shrugged. 'Maybe. Don't worry though – he won't wake until the new moon. And we're almost through now. Tumber's beyond this valley . . .' She looked up, frowning. 'Did you hear that?'

Hercufleas strained his ears, catching the snap of twigs, the dry rustle of dead leaves.

'The wind?' he said hopefully.

Greta shook her head. 'There is no wind,' she said, turning round and edging Artifax into the clearing. 'Something's in the trees.'

'Is it wolves?' he whimpered, cowering up her sleeve. 'A black bear? Or a grizzly squirrel?'

'Quiet,' she hissed, pulling on the reins. Artifax reared up. Suddenly Greta's axe was in her hands.

'Who's there?' she called.

16

The *shuffle-snap-swish* grew louder. Hercufleas began muttering *The Plea of the Flea* over and over, very fast.

Greta peered into the darkness around them. The trees were so thick and the light so faint she could barely see.

'What is it, Greta? A rattlesnoak? Don't let it get us! Fight it, chop it into matchsticks, do something!'

'Can't fight what you can't see,' she murmured.

From her bag she pulled out a long white stick and a small silver tinderbox with a pair of tweezers hanging from the lid on a chain. Hercufleas felt heat coming from it. Around it, the air hummed.

With the tweezers, Greta opened the box a crack, drawing out a living flicker of flame.

A tinderfly! It crackled and popped like a tiny ember.

Before it burned her fingers, Greta pressed the bug down on the sugarstick. With the wick, she tied the fly in place. It buzzed there, an angry blue, until it melted the sugar below. All at once, it settled down to eat. Its wings began to burn a warm, contented orange. A smell of caramel filled the air. Greta shut the tinderbox and held the flame up to the dark.

She called out again. 'Whatever you are, come out!'

Suddenly something enormous burst out of the undergrowth towards them. Greta's skin goosebumped with terror. Hercufleas screamed. He wasn't ready to fight Yuk yet! He wasn't ready to die! He'd only just started to live! He was so terrified, he pooed a tiny rust-red scab onto Greta's wrist (since fleas drink only blood, scabs are what they poo).

But the dark shape wasn't the giant.

In a way, it was worse.

Greta swung the tinderfly around to illuminate Onk-Onk skidding to a stop, his snout snuffling their scent on the ground.

Ugor stepped off his pig, holding his Bazuka, a rifle from the Orient that fired tiny sticks of dynamite. 'Move and you die,' he growled, pointing the gun at them.

'Good sniffing, Onk-Onk.' Keeping his eyes on Greta, he called over his shoulder through the trees, 'She is here, Mr Stickler. With the flea too.'

Mr Stickler appeared behind Ugor, the house-hat on his head like a lantern. Every window was dazzlingly lit – Hercufleas threw his arm across his eyes. When at last he could look, his fleamily were all crowded on the brim holding candles, waving at Hercufleas.

Suddenly they were all yelling:

'Don't worry!'

'You're safe now!'

'Ugor told us what happened!'

'Mr Stickler said you'd probably been kidnapped!'

'We took a boat to cut her off!'

'Min says you can pick *two* bottles from the pantry for dinner!'

Seeing them, Hercufleas sighed in relief. Despite everything, his fleamily were all right. Everything was going to be OK.

Then he remembered that Stickler and Ugor were there too and he realised that wasn't true at all.

'Don't worry, little one!' Min called to Hercufleas. 'We won't let her steal you to sell to some flea circus!'

'That's not what she's doing,' Hercufleas called. 'That isn't what happened!'

But Stickler was speaking too, and his loud voice drowned out Hercufleas. 'You tried to blackmail me,' he said to Greta. 'Then you murdered Prince Xin. Stole Artifax. Kidnapped one of my employfleas. Now you will face justice.'

Greta urged Artifax back to the edge of the clearing, swinging her light from Stickler to Ugor.

'Yes, I'm a thief,' she said. 'A kidnapper too. But I didn't murder Prince Xin. *He* tried to murder *me*! And *you* told him to do it!'

'Kill her, Ugor,' Stickler said with a sigh, picking dirt from under his fingernails. 'Kill her now. We don't need to listen to any of her lies.'

'Wait!' Min cried. 'What about my hatchling?'

Under the hat's brim, the lenses of Stickler's scopical glasses glinted as he thought. 'Hercufleas,' he said at last, 'jump away from that murdering villain now. Ugor needs to dynamite her.'

Greta looked down at Hercufleas. 'He'll tell you the truth!'

Stickler hesitated. On the brim of his hat, the fleamily were looking at each other with puzzled faces.

'What's she talking about, Hercufleas?' asked Pin.

Hercufleas opened his mouth, about to explain everything: the flyte, Prince Xin's fall, Onk-Onk's sneeze, the escape across the lake.

But then, behind Stickler's back, Ugor swung his gun away from Greta.

He pointed it at the house-hat instead.

'Well?' said Stickler. 'Are you going to tell us or not?'

'Go on,' Ugor sniggered. 'Tell them the truth.' And

there was something else the villain said, but only with his eyes: *Tell them the truth, and your fleamily will die.*

'Hercufleas?' said Min. 'What are you waiting for?'

Hercufleas gulped. His brain, the size of a poppy seed, was completely overwhelmed. What should he do? He looked at Greta. Looked at his fleamily. Looked at Ugor's Bazuka. If he was a true, giant-slaying hero, he'd find a way to save the day.

But he was a flea, and just one day old, and he was afraid.

'I saw who murdered Prince Xin,' he said. 'It was . . . It was Greta.'

Ugor nodded and grinned, his gun moving back towards Artifax. 'See? Is just like Ugor tell you. She thief. She kidnapper. She murderer.'

Greta shot Hercufleas a look of such venom he thought he might die from it. 'I believed in you,' she said.

'It's over,' said Stickler curtly. 'Employfleas, go back inside. I've no wish for you to see what happens next.'

Min nodded at the fleamily. They hopped in through the windows and drew the black velvet curtains, but she stayed on the brim of the hat. The clearing was dark again, except for Greta's tinderfly, crackling on its sugarstick.

'Please,' Min begged, 'please give us Hercufleas back.'

93

'You can have him.' Greta scowled. 'I don't ever want to see him again.'

Balling Hercufleas in her fist, she chucked him at Stickler. He was mid-air when her other hand untied the wick and freed the tinderfly. It flew into the sky like an ember from a bonfire, taking the light with it, plunging them into darkness.

17

Shouts and screams in the night. Grunts and squeals. Shrieks and then a *BANG* as Ugor fired his Bazuka. A tiny dynamite stick arced through the air, hissing like a firework.

Then the hissing stopped.

BOOM!

Like a photographer's flash, the fireball illuminated the woodn't for an instant. The shock wave slammed into Hercufleas, cracking every joint in his armour, knocking the breath from his lungs. He saw Stickler blown off his feet, Ugor flung from his pig, and the trees beside them bursting into splinters. He hit the ground, sucking tiny sips of breath, the explosion ringing in his ears.

'Did Ugor get her?' the barbarian shouted, stomping around the burning trees. 'Did Ugor get her?'

Hercufleas's night vision came back slowly, but Artifax and Greta had vanished from the clearing.

I wanted to help you, he thought, wishing she could hear. But I couldn't sacrifice my fleamily.

'My employfleas!' Stickler shrieked, hands prodding the top of his head.

Where the house-hat had sat, there was now just a sizzled bald spot, gently smouldering. The blast had blown it clean off Stickler's head.

And now there was a second explosion, only this one happened inside Hercufleas's heart. Where were Min and Pin? Where were Burp, Slurp, Speck, Fleck, Itch, Titch, Tittle, Dot and Jot? He had loved and left and longed for them – he had betrayed Greta to save them – had he now lost them forever?

'I'm ruined!' blubbed Stickler. 'Happily Ever Afters is done for! Never mind about my reputation, who will type up my P23 hero forms now? Who will even know what a P23 form is?'

'Stop crying,' Ugor told Stickler, giving him a slap. 'Fleas up there. Look.' He pointed at a steep hill, the shape of a dome, that rose behind them. Hercufleas had not noticed it until now, but the pine trees that had obscured it from sight had been blown to matchsticks.

One single tree stood on the top of the hill – the rest was a tangle of vines. The house-hat lay among them, its roof burning. Hercufleas squinted and could just make out the fleamily, passing thimbles of bathtub water to each other as they fought to douse the flames.

Stickler let out a strangled sob. Rushing up to the hill, he gripped the vines and began to climb towards the house-hat. The leaves of the lonely tree on the summit shook. But there was no wind. The air was utterly still.

And yet the tree rattled again. Louder, this time. Angrier.

'STOP!' Hercufleas yelled at Stickler. He leaped up and almost fainted. Pain screeched through him and his arm made a sound like two halves of a broken plate grating together. The impact of the explosion had cracked his armoured skin. But it didn't matter. His fleamily had landed on the lair of a hibernating rattlesnoak, and Stickler was going to wake it up!

The hero's agent swatted at the flames until they fizzled out. Then he seized the house-hat and cuddled it to his chest, while at the top of the hill the rattling from the rattlesnoak seed pods reached a frenzy.

'RUN!' Hercufleas bounded forward, fighting dizziness and pain. 'IT'S WAKING UP!'

Finally Stickler looked down and immediately jumped. The vines around him were moving. They slithered over his feet. One coiled around his ankle. The tip ended in a wide, flat snake head, spade-shaped so it could dig its way up from the ground.

'Ugor?' called Stickler nervously. 'Get this *thing* off my leg.'

With a hiss, the rattleroot sank its fangs into his foot.

Stickler screamed and kicked with his leg, trying to shake it off. 'Ugor! Quick! Get it off!' But the paralysing poison was already starting to work. 'Gerrit oh me! Whash go-ee on, why my shpeeki lie this?'

'HURRY UP!' Hercufleas yelled at the barbarian, as Ugor fumbled another mini-dynamite stick into his Bazuka. It wasn't Stickler he cared about. 'JUMP OVER HERE!' he yelled at his fleamily.

Stickler finally reached down and ripped the rattleroot from his foot. Slurring nonsense, he shuffled up the hill to the rattlesnoak trunk. In his delirious state, he must have thought climbing the tree would give him safety. More rattleroots dug their way to the surface and began to swarm towards him. Hercufleas hopped up and down, screaming for Stickler to hurry and Ugor to fire, powerless to do anything but watch.

Stickler dragged himself up the rattlesnoak trunk, using the boles and crevices in the bark for handholds. The poison had completely paralysed his left leg. He balanced the house-hat on the first branch and then clung there, his strength ebbing away, while the ground below him seethed with rattleroots.

Then Ugor fired the Bazuka, and a fizzing stick of TNT struck the hill with an enormous *BOOM!* The rattleroots dug back under the earth for protection as the shock wave slammed into Hercufleas, making his cracked arm buzz in pain.

The explosion rumbled on and on. Why wasn't it stopping? The earth still trembled. All around the clearing, dry leaves and twigs and clods of mud and pebbles bounced up and down, as if everything was becoming a flea. Had Ugor's dynamite started an earthquake?

The rattlesnoak lurched up into the air – the hill was growing *bigger*. The earth under Hercufleas split and he almost fell into the crack. It was as if the world was turning inside out. Earth and rocks split and tilted. Tree stumps lurched over.

Four enormous *things* burst from the ground over by Onk-Onk, then a fifth. The pig squealed and ran away from the fingers as they wriggled in the air. The rest of the giant hand worked its way up from the earth. The rattlesnoak hill was not a hill at all. It was the top of a head, with two rotten yellow swamps of eyes and fat pupils sitting in the middle of each one like toads and a mouth spitting out mud and roots.

'Giant!' Ugor roared, frantically reloading his Bazuka. 'Giant!'

Hercufleas gazed at Yuk rising and rising until he was high as a mountain. This must be where he went each month to sleep – he buried himself below the woodn't.

Ugor's dynamite had woken him up early.

And he looked very, very angry.

'YUK GUZZLE.'

18

Without thinking, Hercufleas attacked.

'Whatever size his enemies, the winner's always HERCUFLEAS!' he screamed.

His next leap brought him down on the crag of Yuk's knee. The giant's flesh was bark and mud and rock, held together by white roots running through his body like veins. He bounded up the body – from knee to thigh to hip. His broken arm throbbed; he could barely breathe. After a few jumps, his legs were so tired and stretched they felt like old elastic underpants, ready to fall off his bottom. But he kept going. He had to. His fleamily were on the rattlesnoak that sprouted from the giant's head.

Words tumbled down from Yuk's lips like a mudslide.

'WHAT ITCH YUK'S HEAD?'

A giant hand flew up past Hercufleas to grope around the rattlesnoak branches.

'HEY!' Hercufleas bellowed from Yuk's waist, try to distract him. 'DOWN HERE!'

His voice faded into the cool night air. He had to try something else. Leaping sideways, he landed in the cave of Yuk's bellybutton. It was choked with bramble-strangle. Bats roosted in nooks above his head, swooping and shrieking. He ignored them, frantically searching the floor, sensing tender nerve clusters just under the skin like landmines. All fleas instinctively avoid biting the most sensitive parts of their host. But now Hercufleas went for the tenderest spot in Yuk's bellybutton.

And chomped down as hard as he possibly, possibly could.

'OOOOOH!' A roar echoed around the bellybutton. 'WHAT ITCH YUK'S BELLY?'

Hercufleas had one brief moment of triumph. He'd done it! He'd bought his fleamily some time—

Suddenly bats were all around him – a black cloud of panic, fighting to get outside. Hercufleas dodged their flurry of wings and jaws and claws. What had spooked them?

Too late, he saw.

Yuk's giant finger was rushing up the bellybutton towards him. Of course: he'd bitten, now Yuk would scratch the itch.

Right where he stood.

The finger slammed down on him. Crushing. Pulverising. Hercufleas felt his armoured skin crack and pop under the pressure. He tensed his whole body as hard as he could. Trying to stay strong. Trying to survive. He couldn't get squished.

At last he felt the pressure lift, but he was lifted up too. Out of the bellybutton. He was wedged in the gunk and sludge under Yuk's nail. Glued to the end of the giant's fingertip. A crushed and broken bug.

With his last ounce of strength, Hercufleas kicked out with his legs. He wrenched himself free, the gunk stretching like a bungee cord. *Snap!* He tumbled down into the clearing, smearing down a tree trunk until he came to a stop. Stuck.

The giant went back to rummaging around his head. His fingertips brushed the branch where the house-hat sat. Hercufleas watched from below, whispering *The Plea of the Flea*, praying for a miracle. In Avalonian fairy tales, this was the moment when the knight in shining armour appeared and saved the day . . .

Yuk's fingers plucked up Stickler first. 'YUM YUM.' He spoke like Ugor: slow and stupid and cruel. 'YUK NOT NEED TO GUZZLE TOWN FOR TASTY SNACK. TASTY SNACK COME TO YUK.'

Yuk smiled at Stickler, wriggling like a worm in his grip, then tossed the hero-seller onto his tongue. Stickler sloshed around the giant's mouth, trying desperately to paddle away from the gnashing stone teeth, clinging to Yuk's tonsils . . .

Then something flew up from the woodn't like a firework, punching into Yuk's chest. *BOOM!*

In the burning clearing stood the silhouette of Ugor and his Bazuka.

Yuk toppled – it seemed to take hours – and slammed down into the woodn't. The impact made the giant choke and cough up into the air a shining glob of spit. Floating inside it, like a pickled egg in brine, was Mr Stickler. He rose up, slowed, stopped – and fell straight down again into Yuk's mouth. The giant swallowed him with a gulp.

'Onk-Onk, now you fire too!' Ugor bellowed.

As Yuk lurched to his feet, the pig charged, snout belching fire and flames. Two cannonballs hit Yuk with a thud. The giant staggered back, but didn't fall. Not this time. He lunged forward to snatch the barbarian and his pig, cramming them into his mouth.

'TASTE LIKE CHICKEN,' he said.

Hercufleas scanned Yuk's mohican tree for the house-hat . . . There! The impact of the giant's fall had wedged it between two branches. A few of the windows still shone faintly, like a cluster of fallen stars.

Hercufleas cried out for Min and Pin and all the others. Jump, jump, they had to jump now, before it was too late! But his shouts were too small, and came from too far away.

Yuk patted his belly. A burp erupted from his lips, sending the leaves around Hercufleas trembling.

'THAT GOOD GUZZLE,' he said. 'YUK FULL. NOW YUK NEED SLEEP. SOMEWHERE HE NOT GET WOKEN UP BY BIG BOOM-BOOM.'

Hercufleas watched him stomp away. To the horizon and beyond. Carrying the tiny winking lights of the house-hat with him.

19

Hercufleas woke in a matchbox padded with cotton wool. He turned his head and found himself on a windowsill, lying in a sunbeam. Outside was a road strewn with rubble. A wonky sign said 'Merit Street'.

He didn't know where Merit Street was. This wasn't the woodn't, or Avalon, this was somewhere he'd never been. How long had he been asleep? Grimacing, he sat up. Dull pain shot through his broken arm. Someone had sewn up his cracked skin with cotton thread, fixing it back in place. He was mending. Some parts of him, anyway.

There was nothing else to see on the street, so he turned his gaze inwards to the room. It had been a school once. Now half the roof was gone and the desks had rotted in the rain. Old books, swollen with damp, sprouted on the sill beside him like fungi. A faded display lined the far wall – pictures painted in bright colours by little children. Names were printed below them. Ilsa. Ivan. Greta.

This must be Tumber.

Greta's painting was of a small girl, a man, a lady, a donkey and a goat. She'd painted smiley faces on everyone, even the sun.

Hercufleas noticed her then. She was asleep on the floor, curled up by the blackboard, cuddling her axe the way other children cuddle dolls. Hercufleas watched her for a long time. She was having a good dream, he could tell. She was smiling, ever so slightly.

Why hadn't she abandoned him, the way he'd abandoned her?

Down the corridor came the echo of footsteps. An orange glow grew brighter in the doorway. Quickly Hercufleas lay back down in his matchbox and pretended to snore. He kept one eye open. Into the classroom came an old babushka with hair like chicken wire and a tiny copper earring in the shape of a bell. She'd dusted her cheeks with flour and drawn her eyebrows on with charcoal in an attempt to look glamorous. One hand held a walking stick with a brass tip and a carved fox-head handle. In the other, a fat orange tinderfly burned on the stub of a sugarstick.

The babushka looked from Greta to Hercufleas, shaking her head. She muttered something in a language Hercufleas didn't know, setting the tinderfly down. She gave Greta a gentle poke with her stick.

'Five more minutes, Mama,' Greta mumbled.

The babushka sighed and brought her stick down on the floorboards with a sharp crack. Greta groaned. 'Mama, Wuff is barking again.'

The babushka went over to the blackboard and raked her long nails down it. They screeched like broken violins. Greta sat bolt upright, awake and scowling again. She had feathers in her hair from the pillow propped beneath her.

'Wake him,' said the babushka, plucking the feathers out. 'I must tell you what will happen.'

Greta yawned. 'Can't it wait another hour?'

The babushka *tsked*. 'Greta Stump. Even in class you were always with the questions and not with the listening. Less than a month now until Yuk comes back to Tumber, and you wish to sleep? Those he guzzled in the woodn't will not sate his hunger forever.'

'Yeah, Stickler was all greasy and bony,' said Greta. 'Onk-Onk and Ugor were meaty though.'

'Even so. When he returns, this flea is the only hope we have.'

Hercufleas lay still, but his mind raced. *This flea?* Why was the old babushka talking about *him?*

Greta scowled. 'I still say you're wrong about him.'

The babushka *tsked* again and drew her lips into a pencil-thin frown. 'And did you lose your manners when you left for Avalon, along with Tumber's last florins?'

Greta blushed, lowering her head. 'Sorry, Miss Witz.'

Miss Witz put bony hands on bony hips and stared at Hercufleas. He shut his eye quick and made mumbling sounds.

'I wonder,' he heard her mutter. 'I wonder if he really is the one.' She sniffed. 'Let me know when he wakes, child.'

'Yes, Miss Witz.'

Hercufleas heard her leave.

'You know,' said Greta in the silence after Miss Witz had gone, 'I was pretending to be asleep before *you* were pretending to be asleep.'

Hercufleas opened his eyes. He sat up sheepishly.

'You're hungry, I bet,' she said.

His belly gave a hollow growl. He was ravenous!

'I'll take that as a yes,' she said, running her thumb across the blade of her axe. Without wincing, she squeezed a bright bead of red blood into a thimble and plonked it angrily down on the sill beside him.

'Don't choke,' she said sweetly.

Hercufleas glugged the thimble down, trying not to gag. Greta's bitterness was worse than ever – the taste of her anger made his throat raw. He waited for the sweet aftertaste, but it never came. Greta's hope was gone. She no longer believed in him. It wasn't a surprise, after what he'd done. What surprised him was how painful that was. It hurt worse than being crushed by Yuk.

'It wasn't my idea to bring you here,' Greta said in the silence. 'I wanted to leave you behind. Like you left me.'

She bowed her head, tears pattering on the floorboards.

'I'm sorry, Greta. Please don't cry.'

She smiled at that. 'But I'm so good at it,' she said. 'I've had so much practice. We all have. Tumber's other name is the Town of Tears. And I thought you could dry our eyes. I was wrong.'

Hercufleas couldn't meet her icy stare.

'Miss Witz made me go back and find you. She's my

teacher . . . *was* my teacher. Before Yuk guzzled the school. She's the reason you're here, and not still stuck on that tree trunk.' The ice in her voice softened a little. 'Me and Artifax rode back to the clearing. It was easy – we could see the fires from Tumber. And I heard you. Shouting those things, about your fleamily. Saying their names, over and over, like prayers. And then I realised. You might not care about *me*, but you care about *them*, don't you?'

Hercufleas looked up. 'Greta, I . . .'

Her gaze went from icy to burning. 'And Yuk *took them from you*, didn't he?'

Hercufleas nodded, and Greta said very quietly, 'I know how that feels.'

'Greta? Why did Miss Witz make you come back for me?'

She shrugged. 'You'll have to ask her.'

'Ah! Awake are we?' said the old babushka from the door.

Hercufleas jumped. How long had she been there? She was very stealthy for an old granny.

'I am Miss Witz,' she said, hobbling right up to the windowsill. 'And you are Hercufleas. And Greta brought you back from Avalon, the island of heroes. But you are not a hero, are you?'

Hercufleas shook his head. 'No.'

Miss Witz paused, and Greta looked at the copper bell on the babushka's ear, but it did not ring.

'You see, miss? I told you he wasn't. He's not interested in saving Tumber.'

'Pff!' said the babushka. 'It shows only that Hercufleas *believes* he is not. There is a difference. But not a great one. Believe something and it is halfway to being real. Besides, I say, *So what?* Many heroes have come to Tumber before, and all failed to protect us. Yet Hercufleas has bought us some time.' The copper bell rang on her ear, and she smiled. 'Yes, I suppose that isn't strictly true. It was those two villains and that pig who filled Yuk's belly for another month. Now he is gone, sleeping somewhere deep in the woodn't. But as always, he will wake up and come back. So we must prepare to fight once more, and if we win, perhaps Hercufleas will see his fleamily again.'

Hercufleas thought of Min and Pin and the others, in that broken-down house-hat on Yuk's head. Miss Witz was right. If they could survive up there for a month, the giant would bring them back to Tumber when he next came to guzzle.

'But we are getting ahead of ourselves,' Miss Witz

said. 'Hercufleas, you must tell me – if you are not a hero . . . who are you?'

Greta scowled. 'I'll tell you who he is,' she said. 'A coward. A liar. A weakling.'

'I did not ask you, Greta.'

Hercufleas stood on the windowsill, looking at his reflection, searching it for an answer. It stared back, blank-eyed. Who was he? A sad little sultana-sized flea with a cracked arm and a broken heart, sitting on the windowsill.

'I'm alone,' he said.

'I see,' said Miss Witz. 'And now that you know what you are missing, you can tell me what you want.'

Once, Hercufleas would have cried out, *Adventures!* But he was not a little hatchling any more.

'I want my fleamily back,' he said, turning to look at Miss Witz and Greta. 'I want to stop Yuk from taking anyone away, ever again. But how can I do that?'

Miss Witz said very solemnly, 'That is the question that only your quest will answer.'

'Quest?' Greta shook her head. 'Is this a joke? Why isn't your bell ringing? Heroes go on quests. Hercufleas isn't a hero!'

'Good,' Miss Witz said. 'No hero can defeat Yuk,

because no hero can wield a weapon big enough to destroy him. To Yuk, Excalibur is a toothpick. An arrow from Rama's bow is a pinprick. Ugor's Bazuka did nothing much. A blade big enough to chop off Yuk's head would need to be many houses high. Who could lift such a thing? This is what Greta made me realise, the night she stole the florins and went to Avalon seeking a *giant-slayer*. And she found one: you.'

'Me?' Hercufleas groaned. 'Haven't you been listening to Greta? I'm not a giant-slayer. I'm just a flea.'

Miss Witz's face wrinkled into a smile. 'Which is very lucky indeed. For a flea is exactly what Tumber needs.'

Hercufleas looked up. 'It is?'

'Yes. Because there is only one weapon capable of destroying Yuk. And only a flea can wield it.'

Miss Witz sat on the desk by Greta and took from her pockets two knitting needles and a tangle of wool. In her lap she began knitting her wool into a green scarf; in the air, she began weaving her words into a story.

20

'Long ago,' Miss Witz began, 'your ancestors, Hercufleas, were more than just pests. They made a name for themselves as the greatest giant-slayers of all. Across the world fleas went, killing humans who were ten thousand times their size. To people, fleas were like grains of sand, yet they killed them with a single nip of their fangs.'

Hercufleas looked at Greta. Were fleas really once so mighty? It sounded like a fairy tale.

'It's true,' Miss Witz whispered hoarsely, 'every word I say. And you may wonder, Hercufleas, why your ancestors killed with a single bite and you cannot. The answer, I tell you, is this: you do not have the weapon that they carried.'

She paused. The only sounds were the tinderfly's

buzzing and her needles clack-clacking together.

'This weapon was not a sword, or an axe, or a Bazuka, or a bow,' she continued. 'It was a plague. The deadliest disease of all. And its name was the Black Death.'

Greta breathed in sharply. Beside her, Hercufleas felt her prickle of fear.

'The Black Death,' repeated Miss Witz, shivering. 'Carrying this weapon inside them, your tiny ancestors killed millions upon millions of people.' She smiled grimly. 'Fleas killing humans . . . Tell me, Hercufleas, what is that, if not giant-slaying?'

'But the Black Death is gone,' Greta blurted out. 'It doesn't exist any more.'

'Ah,' said Miss Witz. 'For the answer to that, I must finish my story. The Black Death was a dreadful weapon, yes, but it had one weakness: feeding on death and destruction, it had to constantly kill to survive. Eventually it became too deadly. Killing too quickly, before it had a chance to spread. And so the plague destroyed itself and humanity survived. And yet . . .

'Even after all that suffering and loss, some saw the terrible power of the Black Death, and wanted that power for themselves. Evil men, who loved to conquer and kill – warlords, emperors, generals. One of them was the old king of Petrossia.'

'The Czar,' Greta breathed, and Hercufleas remembered the portrait on the stamp above the stairs back in the house-hat. The man with the smouldering eyes.

'The Czar.' Miss Witz nodded. 'The most fearsome,

bloodthirsty king Petrossia has ever known, and he did not see the danger of the Black Death; only its power. Sacrificing whole armies, he managed to take a single drop of the Black Death and contain it within a phial. Then he sealed the phial in a lead box, placed the lead box in a stone chest and put the stone chest in the heart of his great fortress in the northern Waste. And then he told his enemies exactly where it was.'

'Why would he do that?' said Hercufleas.

'To terrify them,' said Miss Witz. 'To let them know he had the most dreadful weapon in all the world, and that he could unleash it at any time. Knowing this, who would be mad enough to attack him? Now, of course, the Czar has been dead for many years, murdered in mysterious circumstances. His fortress has fallen to ruin . . . yet there the Black Death remains.'

'No one can take it,' said Greta. 'Because anyone who opens that phial . . .'

' . . . will die from the Black Death themselves.' Miss Witz nodded again.

'Except for me,' said Hercufleas.

Greta looked down at him. At last Miss Witz stopped knitting. Curled up in her lap was a finished green scarf.

'Except for you,' she said. 'Like all fleas, you are

immune. You can carry the Black Death without being harmed by it yourself. Go to the Czar's old fortress, Hercufleas. Find the chest. Open the lead box. Break the phial. Drink the drop inside. Then we will have our weapon – the only weapon that can defeat Yuk.'

'Miss Witz!' Greta hugged her teacher. 'You're a genius! He really *is* a giant-slayer!'

But Hercufleas didn't feel like one. Something nasty coiled inside him, like a drop of cobra blood. 'You don't just want me to defeat Yuk,' he said to Miss Witz. 'You want me destroy him. *Kill* him.'

'Yuk kills,' Greta said, whirling round, 'and he'll keep on killing. If you don't do this, it will be *your* fault when he guzzles everyone in Tumber.'

Miss Witz leaned down, joints cracking like snapped pencils, until her chin was resting on the windowsill. 'Greta is right,' she said. 'I wish there was another way. We are at the end of our hope here in Tumber. It all comes down to you. I have never begged for anything before, but I am begging you now.' She clasped her mottled blue hands together. 'Please, Hercufleas. Please. Save us.'

21

There was no time to lose. Somewhere to the north was a fortress, and inside that fortress was the only weapon that could stop Yuk, a weapon only Hercufleas could carry.

'Every hero must go on a quest to find their weapon,' Miss Witz said as she carried him out of the school. 'Roland of Breton received his sword, Durendal, from an angel. Albion's Arthur pulled Excalibur from a stone. The vorpal sword that killed the Jabberwock was—'

'But how do I get *my* weapon?' said Hercufleas.

'You must go far to the north. Beyond the great lakes we call the Sorrows, somewhere in the endless tundra of the Waste. Find the fortress. Travel to its heart. Bring the Black Death back to Tumber.'

Hercufleas tried not to tremble. This was what he'd wanted ever since he'd hatched – a real adventure, with real danger. But now it was happening, he wasn't excited. He just felt sick and scared.

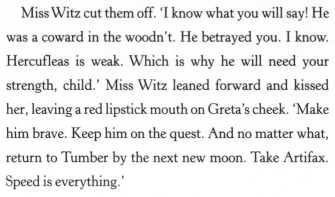

'You will need help,' said Miss Witz, taking the green scarf she'd knitted and draping it around Greta's neck. 'Go with him, Greta.'

'*Me?*' Greta gawped.

So did Hercufleas. '*Her?*'

Miss Witz cut them off. 'I know what you will say! He was a coward in the woodn't. He betrayed you. I know. Hercufleas is weak. Which is why he will need your strength, child.' Miss Witz leaned forward and kissed her, leaving a red lipstick mouth on Greta's cheek. 'Make him brave. Keep him on the quest. And no matter what, return to Tumber by the next new moon. Take Artifax. Speed is everything.'

Greta scowled at Hercufleas, then stormed off to pack.

'Isn't there someone else I could go with?' he asked hopefully. 'What about you, Miss Witz?'

She cackled, thumping her walking stick on the path.

'I am too old, dear little flea.' She watched Greta leave, adding quietly, 'And do not think it is just *her* who will be helping *you*. For Greta is also on a quest – yes, she is. To find a way to heal her heart, which was broken by Yuk many guzzlings ago.' The old babushka sighed. 'She did not used to scowl so much, you know. When she was a child, she did nothing but smile.'

'She's still a child,' said Hercufleas.

Miss Witz smiled sadly, because her copper bell was ringing. 'Maybe.' She left him there and started off down the road. 'Now I will go tell our plan to the survivors.'

Two hours later, Greta and Hercufleas rode Artifax out of Tumber. It was sunset and the blue stars winked on, one after the other, across the violet sky.

In the town the warm orange street lamps formed constellations of their own. The ruined church of Saint Katerina was silent on the hill. Artifax trotted past house after empty house. Hercufleas read their names: Old Barrow, Stove Cottage, the Saltpots. Each one beaten up, like boxers gone ten rounds too many. Doorways gaping, windows knocked out. Nobody home.

'Where is everyone?' Hercufleas asked.

'Guzzled,' said Greta. 'These are the dead streets.

There aren't many of us left.'

They stopped by the houses of the cinderwikk men, with their singed fingers and tinted goggles, who bred tinderflies to fill Tumber's street lamps. Greta refilled her silver tinderbox, taking a stack of sugarsticks too. She broke off a nub from one and popped it in Artifax's beak.

At last they reached the bridge called Two Tears, where the river separated the town from the woodn't beyond. Miss Witz had spread word of the new hero, and a small crowd gathered behind her to see him off. Most of the surviving Tumberfolk were there. As well as the cinderwikk men, there were the bakers of Butterbröt Lane; cossack hunters with huskies, curly pipes and long knotted beards; the roost-wives, who braided their hair into baskets to hold chickens on their heads; and Mayor Klare, with his ledger and quill.

Hercufleas shook his head. So few people for such a big town.

'Good Tumberfolk, I present to you . . . our hero!' Miss Witz announced as Artifax drew close. 'Small he may be, but—'

'Good gracious!' said a roost-wife. 'He's a giant chicken!'

'No,' said Hercufleas. 'That's Artifax. He's helping me.'

'Is that a talking earwig?' said a baker, pointing at Hercufleas.

'I believe he's a woodlouse,' corrected Mayor Klare.

'No,' said Hercufleas nervously, hopping onto Artifax's head so the crowd could see him. 'I'm a flea.'

The astonished Tumberfolk strained their ears to hear his words.

'What did it say?' someone whispered.

'It said it was a bee.'

'It doesn't *look* like a bee.'

Hercufleas rolled his eyes. 'A flea, not a bee.'

'He's not a bee!' Greta shouted.

'Then why did he *say* he was a bee?' someone called back.

'He's certainly acting very suspiciously for a woodlouse,' said Mayor Klare. He was a thin man with a bald, bobbing head, a beaky nose and skin pink as a baby's. Round his neck was a golden key threaded through a red ribbon. On his shoulders was a black cloak. In his hands was a white goose-feather quill. Tucked under his arm was a brown ledger, containing all the laws of Tumber, and the punishments for breaking them.

'He's not a woodlouse either!' Greta yelled.

'Whatever he is,' said a loud voice, 'he doesn't look

much like a hero.'

The words came from a house beside the crowd. A woman stood above them, framed in an open window. She resembled a portrait of an extremely fat, very cruel queen – one who enjoyed beheading her subjects. Probably while eating éclairs.

'Mrs Lorrenz!' Miss Witz's voice was sharp as a pin jab. 'Heroes are like the cakes you bake. To make them, you must follow a precise recipe.'

'He looks like he's missing a few ingredients to me,' sniped Mrs Lorrenz. 'About 250 pounds of muscle, for one. I've made truffles bigger than him!'

'You're right,' Hercufleas called out to the Tumberfolk. 'Greta had to kidnap me to come here. And when she was in trouble, I betrayed her. That's why I'm going on this quest. I'm not a hero yet, but I want to be. I'm going to try. And I promise I'll never give up.'

Mayor Klare gawped. Mrs Lorrenz turned the colour of cream. The Tumberfolk went quiet.

'That,' said Mayor Klare, 'was the least heroic speech I've ever heard. And I've heard a few. We haven't got a chance!'

'We're doomed,' whimpered Mrs Lorrenz, slumping on the windowsill like a collapsed blancmange.

Uh oh. Hercufleas looked around at the panicking faces. The Tumberfolk didn't want to hear the truth, he realised too late. They wanted nice, comforting lies about how everything was going to be all right.

Mayor Klare rounded on Greta. 'This is all the child's fault!' he told the crowd. '*She* stole the last florins in the treasury. Have we forgotten? She is a thief, and thieves must be punished!'

Miss Witz cracked her cane on the cobbles. 'Listen to me—'

'According to the laws of Tumber,' said the mayor, consulting his ledger, 'thieves are required to wear a special hat fitted with a wind chime, so we know where they are at all times.'

Greta scowled. 'Nice speech,' she hissed at Hercufleas, spurring Artifax past the startled mayor. They sped away through the crowd and over the bridge. Greta dropped two tears down into the water, then they were off into the woodn't. The town vanished behind them, but whenever Hercufleas closed his eyes he could still see the despairing faces of the crowd. The cries of Mayor Klare and Mrs Lorrenz echoed around his head.

We haven't got a chance.

We're doomed.

22

Artifax picked his way through the woodn't, guided by Greta past the seed-shaking rattlesnoaks. Once, they had to outrun a grizzly squirrel that caught their scent.

They headed north, always north. The Czar's fortress lay somewhere beyond the Sorrows, in the frozen Waste. Hercufleas tried not to think about where they were going and what he would have to do there. The idea of drinking the drop of Black Death made him shiver, even more than the increasing cold. He snuggled in the folds of Greta's green scarf, nipping her awake whenever her head nodded down on her chest.

After many hours, even Artifax was too exhausted to carry on. They took shelter beneath a tree. Hercufleas glanced up at the branches.

'Are you sure this one's not . . . hungry?' he asked.

But Greta was already asleep, cuddling her axe. All night in her sleep she mumbled about everpines, green giants and gardens of the world.

Next day they passed the first of the Sorrows, the great salt lakes where nothing could live. These lay between the mountains like shards of fallen sky. Greta explained how they got their name.

'It comes from one of the old prophecies. God adds one salty tear to the lakes for every new evil in the world. But the prophecy's end has been lost, so people argue about what happens next. Miss Witz says a day is coming when evil will be gone and life will return to the Sorrows. Mayor Klare says that soon God will add so

many tears the lakes will overflow and flood Petrossia with bitterness.'

'Whose ending do you believe?' Hercufleas asked.

Greta gave a short bitter laugh. 'I don't believe in anything.'

Gradually the landscape changed. The lifeless Sorrows disappeared. Beyond them, the everpines grew more sparse, until the woodn't became a featureless grey tundra. There were still brambleberries for Artifax to eat, but they were black and sour. Greta dug up particular roots, mashing them into a bitter paste for her supper, but then the trees changed and she no longer knew which ones were safe to eat.

They were too far from home.

Every evening Greta pricked her finger with a pin, squeezing a drop of blood into a thimble for Hercufleas to drink. It tasted more bitter each time. He felt miserable for hours afterwards. He tried drinking Artifax's blood instead, but the morning after he woke up squatting on the ground trying to lay an egg, so he stopped.

It grew bitterly cold. In the mornings Greta's blanket and scarf were stiff with ice and Artifax's feathers glittered with tiny diamonds of frost. Hercufleas woke so frozen he couldn't move. Greta had to cup him in her hands and blow steaming breath, like a tiny sauna, until his limbs softened.

The deeper they went into the Waste, the less Greta spoke. Silence layered over her, like ice. A scowl froze solid on her face and wouldn't thaw.

Hercufleas talked endlessly, trying to break through to her. She just buried her chin in her scarf and ignored him, as he chattered about his fleamily and life before the adventure. It was hard, because that had only been one day, so he kept running out of memories. But thinking back to when he was an egg, he remembered all the sounds that had passed through his shell.

He remembered hearing Burp and Slurp sneak down

to the pantry for midnight feasts. And Tittle, who liked to sing, but would only do it under the kitchen table when she thought no one was listening. Or Dot, who used to talk to him endlessly, trying to convince him that he should hatch out as a girl, not a boy.

He missed them all. Just talking about the tall stacks of blood in the pantry or remembering the boingy-boing room seemed to make him feel warmer.

But nothing could melt Greta. Hour after hour, she grew colder. Artifax was suffering too. Since entering the Waste, his feathers had faded from white to grey. Not even bits of sugarstick could cheer him now. He was so weak, they were barely plodding along.

Three days from Tumber, they saw a black castle in the distance.

'That's not it,' said Hercufleas. Miss Witz had told them the Czar's fortress was star-shaped – the castle ahead of them was a square jumble of turrets.

But Greta's whoop echoed around the bleak hills, and she spurred Artifax into a gallop. 'Shelter!' she cried, her silence cracking at last. 'Fires! Food! Maybe even a hot bath!'

But the black castle was a deserted ruin. There were signs of a great battle, years past, but only vines scaled

133

the walls now, toppling them one by one.

'Hello?' called Greta. 'Anyone?'

A rusty gate screeched as the wind blew it open and shut, open and shut. Entering the keep, they saw the murder-holes above their heads. This was one of the Czar's old castles, where he stationed his armies, or perhaps imprisoned his enemies.

'We can still shelter here,' said Hercufleas. 'Keep out of the wind.'

But something about the place scared Artifax. Cold and shivering as he was, he wouldn't stay inside the keep. Greta said nothing, but that night Hercufleas tasted something fresh and black in her blood. It was despair, and it filled him too.

They began to pass more ruined castles – barbicans and kremlins and ostrogs. This was the frozen heart of Petrossia, once the centre of the Czar's empire.

They were so close.

That night, out in the Waste, was the coldest yet. They huddled together – Hercufleas in Greta's hands, and Greta under Artifax's wing – while the boreal winds howled around them like wolves, gnawing at their bones. Above, the aurora shifted from emerald to violet to colours that have no name and cannot be seen. But neither Greta nor Hercufleas craned their heads skyward to watch, for nothing can be beautiful to those with despair in their heart.

Next morning, drifting in the wind like ghosts, they came upon a frozen lake. It stretched in front of them like a quarry of blue marble. Greta edged Artifax across it, testing the ice with each step.

'This isn't like the Sorrows,' she whispered. 'Something actually lives in here. The nomads that follow the reindeer herds across the Waste must stop here – look.'

She pointed. There were old fishing holes in the ice.

'We have to catch something,' she trembled, stiff fingers unravelling a long ball of twine from her pocket. 'Artifax won't survive another night on berries and roots. Not when it's this cold.'

Hercufleas looked at the poor bird, and saw it was true. Artifax had grown shiveringly thin, with frost dripping from his beak. Prince Xin had bred him for beauty and speed, not for weather like this.

'There's just one problem though,' said Greta.

'What?'

'We need bait.'

Why was she staring at him?

135

'Oh no!' He jumped backwards, waving his hands. '*Me*? Not *me*! Why *me*?'

'Because you're a fat, tasty bug,' Greta said, grinning for the first time in ages. 'Relax. I'll tie you to the line, yank out any fish that bites, and cut you from its belly in a flash.'

She actually wanted him to get swallowed whole? 'No. No way.' He pointed at her satchel. 'Use a tinderfly!'

'I won't.' Her grin dropped off her face like an icicle. 'They're precious.' She scowled.

'*I'm* precious!'

'I only have five of them left.'

'You only have *one* of me! I'm the *hero*!'

'Prove it.' She laid a hand on Artifax, who gave a miserable cluck and buried his head under his wing. 'Do something heroic, something that tells me all this cold and hunger is worth it.'

She stomped off to sharpen her axe, leaving Hercufleas staring down at the dark hole in the ice. He gulped. What might swim down there? How sharp were its teeth? He pushed the thoughts from his head. Greta was right. If he couldn't face a fish, how would he fight Yuk?

Hopping over to the twine, he looped it around his waist, double-treble-super-tight.

'Go on then,' he called. 'Let's go fishing.'

Greta took up the line. She dangled him above the ice hole. 'Take a deep breath,' she said. 'Give three tugs when you want to come up.'

Hercufleas nodded as she lowered him down. There was a snapping sound (like when you break a biscuit in two) as he split the thin rime of ice covering the hole. Then a sploshing sound (like when you dunk a biscuit into a mug of tea) as he fell into the black depths of the lake.

23

It was like plunging into an alchemist's cauldron and slowly turning to lead. There was a flash of unspeakable cold, then Hercufleas went numb. The freezing water turned his arms and legs into dead weights. His eyes were heavy but he forced them open. Bubbles escaped his lips as his jaw dropped.

Above his head, the ice was a glowing, crystal sky. Greta's feet were two dark smudges, like angry clouds. On either side the water stretched away to a dark blue blur, with shafts of light coming down from the other ice holes. It was still and beautiful and utterly lifeless. No fish anywhere. Perhaps this place was like the Sorrows after all.

Hercufleas reached to tug the line so Greta could hoist him up. They'd have to find food somewhere else.

Then something moved. He didn't see it, just felt it.

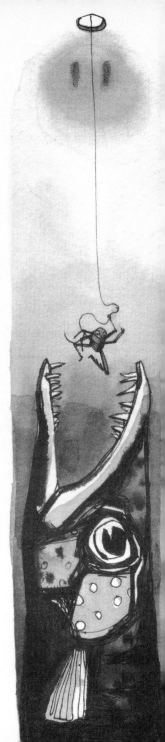

The water rippled beneath him, sending him bobbing on the line. Hercufleas glanced down into the void below. Nothing but endless black. Unease stirred in his stomach. How deep was this lake? What slithered and wriggled under his feet, out of sight?

He bobbed again. Now he saw the dark water shifting. A long shape was swimming up from the depths. It was big. Really big. This was a bad idea. A very, very bad idea. What if this fish liked to chew its food before it swallowed? What if it was too strong for Greta? What if it yanked too hard and the line broke?

Bubbles flurried past him. Panic took hold. Hercufleas grasped the thread and tugged it three times. Greta yanked him out the lake. He dangled above the hole, sodden and spluttering and shivering, forcing his numb lips to speak.

'F-f-f-f-f-f-f.'

'What's the matter?' she said.

139

'Out of breath? Anything down there?'

'F-f-f-f-f-fi. F-f-f-f-fish.'

Then the fish burst up from the ice hole, snapped its jaws around Hercufleas and swallowed him whole. In a whirl of slime and spit he slooshed down its throat. Halfway down, he jerked to a stop, dangling from the thread. His lifeline. Taut as a piano wire.

Don't break, he prayed. Please don't break. As long as the line held, Greta could pull him out.

Then the fish bit down on the twine and it snapped. Hercufleas fell with a splash into its belly.

He reeked of fish guts for hours afterwards.

'How about I dunk you in the lake again?' Greta offered. 'That'll wash the stink off.'

Hercufleas scowled, shuffling closer to the fire. An enormous fish steak was sizzling slowly on the embers, skin crisp and black. Artifax sat beside the fish's skeleton, belly plump, clucking contentedly in his sleep. Hercufleas looked at the remains again. Compared to him, the fish was the size of a whale.

'Lucky,' Greta said again, staring at the skeleton. 'It jumped out of the hole after you and landed straight on the ice, bouncing and flipping and snapping its jaws.

Artifax leaped on it. Just think – if I hadn't pulled you up when I had, you'd probably still be in its belly.'

She chuckled. Hercufleas said nothing. He stared, shivering, into the flames.

'Know something?' said Greta, cramming flakes of charred fish into her mouth. 'It wasn't just luck. You were pretty heroic too.'

Hercufleas didn't feel heroic, although he couldn't deny that something had changed. Later on, when he began muttering about his fleamily – trying to stop his teeth chattering – Greta actually listened. He told her the story of when Burp drank too much bat blood and spent the next week hanging upside down in the chimney, and she even laughed.

What had changed in her? Sipping her blood that night, he figured it out. Underneath the bitterness was a hint of something sweet, like caramel.

Greta had begun to believe in him again.

Darkness fell quickly, but before the winds came howling down from the north, Greta rubbed Artifax's feathers with the fish's fat. The blubber was white and gloopy and smelled awful, but it kept the wind out and the heat in. They slept that night on the frozen lake, snug as seals.

'Hercufleas, look!'

He woke in the darkness and crawled from her pocket, rubbing his eyes. From underneath Artifax's wing, Greta gazed up at the sky. Stars were falling upon the Waste. Bright and glittering, in their hundreds.

'Shooting stars,' Greta whispered. 'Mama said they each bring a new hope to Earth. If you see one fall, you have to name it quick. Then that hope becomes yours to keep.'

Hercufleas pointed. 'That star there,' he said, 'hopes I never have to be fish bait ever again.'

Greta grinned. 'That star there hopes you stop stinking of guts.'

'That star is going to be disappointed. I'm going to torment your nose until we find the Czar's fortress.'

She laughed. 'Well, *that* star there, then? It hopes we find the fortress tomorrow. Then you can drink the Black Death and we can go home.'

Hercufleas stopped smiling. 'Greta,' he whispered, 'what does the Black Death do?'

She looked down at him, a puzzled looked on her face. 'It kills. Whatever it infects, which is whatever you bite. Thought you knew that.'

He nodded. 'I do, I do.'

They watched the sky together.

'If this was an adventure in a story, we'd be the heroes, wouldn't we?' Hercufleas whispered. 'And Yuk would be the monster?'

Greta nodded fiercely. 'Of course!'

'I thought so.' He sighed. 'In a story, the ones using the Black Death would be the monsters.'

Greta plucked him up in her hand and held him close. Her odd-coloured eyes shone with starlight.

'Yuk's the one that kills,' she told him. 'Yuk. Not us. It's all because of him . . .'

She trailed off. Hercufleas waited. He saw her unpacking the grief from her heart, all the sorrow and hurt, arranging it into a story. Something she could bear to tell.

There, beneath a sky of falling hopes, she told him of her parents.

24

They lived in a cottage where the town met the woodn't. Coming home from school in the evening, Greta could always hear the *whack-whack-whack* of Mama's axe on the stump. Like their home had its own heartbeat.

They had a donkey called Kopotikop, a goat called Potch and a dog called Wuff. Every day he ran to Greta when she rounded the corner with her school book and satchel. Mama would be splitting kindling for the fire, her hair tied back with a scarf. Papa would be inside by the stove, making pies with plumpkin and cheese curdled from Potch's milk.

Greta's job was to make the tea.

The delicacy of Tumber is nettle tea, which other towns cannot drink because of its bitterness. But Tumber is the Town of Tears, and the folk there add a teaspoon of tears of laughter to the pot, and stir, turning the tea sweet.

While Papa cooked and Mama chopped, they told Greta silly stories. Some were tales everyone in Petrossia knew, like 'The Invention of Snow', or 'Why the Green Giants Sleep'. Others were known only by them, like 'The Rattlesnoak called Natalya'.

Greta listened, holding the teaspoon up to catch her happy tears, and before long she had enough to tip in with the nettles and water.

Like everyone, they argued and bickered and infuriated each other from time to time. That is the thing about families. Like snowflakes, they are each entirely different and yet all exactly the same, and though they are innumerable upon the Earth, the loss of each one is a sorrow.

After tea one night, Mama helped Greta tie a tinderfly to a sugarstick and they all took Wuff on a walk. The air was a cold glaucous blue, thick with the smoky smell of the town. A cinderwikk man stood on stilts, filling the street lamps with caramel and tinderflies. One flew free before he could shut the lid. Wuff and Greta chased the buzzing spark all the way to the river, over Two Tears, right to the edge of the woodn't. There Greta stopped, but Wuff ran into the trees.

'Wuff! Wuff, come back, you're not supposed to go in there!'

'That dog,' Mama said, shaking her head. She ruffled Greta's hair. 'Good girl for not following him in though.'

She stomped off to fetch him, while Papa took Greta's hand and led her a few steps in, to show her it was safe.

'See that everpine there?' He pointed. 'Only cut their branches, never their trunk. Evers are gentle trees. They've been here since the green giants planted the first forests on the Waste and turned Petrossia into a garden.'

'Wuff!' Mama called. 'Here, boy! Time to go!'

Greta's eyes went wide. 'Just like in the story?'

Papa nodded. 'Just like in "Why the Green Giants Sleep". It's a true story, that. The oldest, truest story in all Petrossia.'

'Wuff! Wuuuuuff! Come on!'

'And that nasty thing there?' said Papa, reaching forward. 'That's a needler shrub. Pull it out, like this, before it grows too big and starts shooting its needles at the poor birds.'

'Wuff!'

'Papa?' Greta asked. 'Where's Wuff gone?'

Papa looked up and peered into the woodn't. Then he looked up at Mama, and his expression changed. All the warmth went out of it.

'What is it, Papa? Has Wuff got lost?'

He didn't answer. Suddenly his axe was in his hand.

'Black bear?' Greta heard him whisper.

'No,' Mama whispered back. 'Bigger.'

'You haven't got your axe. We should run.'

'Too late. It's already seen us.'

Greta didn't know what they were scared of. But Papa – who'd carved Mama's name into a rattlesnoak – was trembling. That terrified her.

'Go home, Greta,' Mama said.

She folded her arms stubbornly. 'I want Wuff.'

'We'll find him,' said Papa. His voice was soft, like whenever Greta scraped her knee and he pretended it was nothing. 'Go home and make a nice pot of nettle tea, and we'll be back in a bit to drink it. With Wuff.'

'Wuff!' Greta called into the woodn't.

Mama whirled around, eyes blazing, and shoved Greta away. 'Do what your father says. RUN!'

And Greta ran. Across the river, up the street, beneath

the moonless sky. Past Kopotikop and Potch, back into the cottage. She sat weeping into a pot of nettle tea like Papa had told her, her frightened tears turning it sour as vinegar.

It didn't matter. Her parents never came back to drink it.

There was a search. The cossacks gave their huskies the scent of Mama's scarf, but the dogs just stayed at the edge of the woodn't, barking at the trail of broken trees that led away from the town. That's when the hunters found the footprints in the soft mud by the river. Footprints a dozen people could lay down in.

That was the first guzzling.

A month later, when the moon was new and the night was darkest, the giant returned to Tumber and ripped the roofs from a whole street of houses. Mayor Klare called a meeting. All the Tumberfolk came. The cossacks wanted to take up arms and go hunt the monster. The cinderwikk men wanted to burn the whole woodn't to the ground. Mrs Lorrenz suggested they all move to Laplönd. But Mayor Klare argued that Tumber could not save itself. Only a hero could protect it.

That night he left for Avalon with the first of the florins.

★

When someone tells you a story like that, everything changes. At the same time, it stays the same. Greta's heart was still full of hurt. Sorrow she couldn't let go of, and wouldn't forgive. But now Hercufleas knew why. He understood her scowls and tears. Why she cradled the axe with the rattlesnoak handle. Why she hated being abandoned.

'I'm sorry I left you to Ugor,' he said quietly. 'He was threatening my fleamily.'

She sniffed. 'You lied to protect them.'

'Are you still angry at me?'

'No. I don't think I ever was angry. I was jealous. Because I couldn't save my Mama and Papa, but you still can.'

Hercufleas looked up. The stars were still falling. Which of the hopes they had named tonight would come true tomorrow? He closed his eyes and went to sleep, not knowing.

When they woke in the morning and climbed the last hill past the lake, though, the answer was there on the horizon. There, on the flat and featureless Waste. Star-shaped, as if it had fallen from the sky the night before.

The Czar's fortress.

25

The Czar's fortress had six towers, twelve walls and one hundred and forty-four turrets, all made from granite. It was an intricate, colossal star, built to withstand any siege or battle. Once it had been a place where dread armies gathered under the smouldering stare of that long-dead king. Now it was a deserted ruin.

As Greta rode Artifax closer and closer, Hercufleas hopped with nerves. All their travelling had come down to this: the single drop of plague in the heart of this fortress.

'We should be careful,' said Greta, snapping him from his thoughts. 'What if some of the Czar's armies are still here? Miss Witz told me the outer walls were defended by Frost Titans that the Czar conquered and forced to serve him.'

'Frost Titans!' Hercufleas whispered. Maybe, if they

were friendly, they could come back to Tumber and fight Yuk in his place.

But as Artifax ran across the vast drawbridge, it became clear the fortress was deserted. The walls either side were pockmarked and scorched from ancient sieges. The iron gate had disintegrated – perhaps from cannonballs, or maybe just from the freezing cold. And no Frost Titans stood upon the battlements.

'They must have been defeated,' Greta said in the eerie silence. 'During a siege of Lava Imps, it looks like. Up there!'

The walls were lined with crumbling statues of terrifying gargoyles. At first Hercufleas thought they were part of the fortress's design, but then he saw they were made of much darker stone. Every one of them was frozen in a posture of battle.

'Looks like the heat of the Lava Imps melted the Frost Titans,' said Greta. 'But at the same time, the Imps were frozen too. Miss Witz said that after the Czar died, all the armies he had conquered began fighting among themselves.'

Hercufleas didn't understand – he thought the fortress had been designed to be impenetrable, but if a few Lava Imps managed to breach it . . .

'It doesn't seem like a very *good* fortress,' he began.

Then he saw.

Inside the walls was *another* fortress, the image of the first, only half the size. It had the same six towers, twelve walls and one hundred and forty-four turrets, but made from white marble rather than black granite.

'A castle inside a castle,' Hercufleas breathed.

'It's like a matryoshka,' said Greta. 'You know, those wooden dolls they sell at the souvenir stalls in Avalon? Each doll is hollow, with a smaller one inside. When they're all stacked together, you can't tell how many there might be.'

Hercufleas gazed at the fortress. 'And how many layers does *this* matryoshka have?'

Greta shrugged. 'Only one way to find out.'

She spurred Artifax on. The white marble fortress was a lifeless ruin too.

'I think this layer was guarded by Cloud Ogres. Look – see the scorch marks from their lightning bolts? They defeated the last of the Lava Imps, but a horde of Wind Wolves attacked soon after and blew them all away.' She shivered. 'Wind Wolves. Sometimes they come into the woodn't. Filled with huff and puff. Papa put a boiling cauldron in the hearth whenever they were prowling outside. He said it stopped them coming down the chimney.'

The next fortress was smaller again, and made of yellow sandstone. It was strewn with broken brass lamps.

'This looks bad.' Greta scowled. 'First the Frost Titans, then the Cloud Ogres and now the Sand Genies. Maybe someone fought past them and took the Black Death long ago.'

She urged Artifax on. Within the sandstone fortress was another made of brass, which Greta said had probably been defended by General Pachelbel and his canons. She found an old rusted Howlitzer in the gatehouse: a blunderbuss weapon used by the Czar to defeat the Orchestras of Hertzenberg. The barrel was made from a gramophone horn, and it fired terrifying screams and howls straight into an enemy's ears. Greta slung it over her shoulder along with her axe.

The fortresses got smaller and smaller in size, until at last they came to one the size of a house, made from red bricks. Unlike the others, there were no breaches in its walls. Its rusty gate was shut.

'No way in,' Greta fumed, stalking around the brick fortress. 'We must be close to the Black Death now.'

'I could jump those walls easily,' Hercufleas said.

'Why don't you wait here?'

Greta gave a snort. 'Artifax could jump them too,' she said. 'He just needs a run-up.'

Pop! Pop! Pop! Tiny puffs of smoke floated up from the red-brick battlements, and Hercufleas saw three black specks whizz towards them. His heart leaped – could it be there were fleas guarding this fortress? Fleas like him?

'Hello?' He looked around for them. 'Where did the fleas go?' he asked Greta.

She looked down at her hand, clutching her side. 'They weren't fleas,' she said.

Artifax reared back and Greta lost her balance and fell. Hercufleas tumbled down with her. They thumped onto the frozen ground. 'Greta?' he said, bouncing up and down on her nose. 'Open your eyes! Are you hurt?'

She didn't answer, but her hand rolled from her side, and he saw blood.

26

Usually, blood made him think *yummy* and *dinner* and *hooray*. Not this blood. It oozed from a wound in Greta's side, red and hot and awful. Those black whizzing things were minute bullets. Something in the red-brick fortress had shot her!

'I'm OK,' she gasped. 'I'm fine.'

'They hurt you!' He hopped up and down with rage. 'They *hurt* you! Now I'm going to hurt them. I'm going to—'

'Calm down,' she winced. 'First you're going to calm down.'

'But they *HURT YOU!*' he roared. His anger was scalding hot; his heart pounded in his chest and his head.

'Only a little bit,' she grunted, squeezing with her fingers at the wound. Out onto her fingertip came a little black ball, the size of a peppercorn. 'Humans are big, Hercufleas. It takes more than a little cut like this to kill us.'

'So you're OK? When you fell off Artifax, I thought . . .'

'I fell off Artifax on purpose,' she said, through gritted teeth. 'To buy us some time. Hercufleas, listen – someone's still guarding the Black Death. They're in that fortress, guns trained on us right now. It'd take dozens of shots like this to kill me and Artifax . . . Whoever's in there isn't stupid. They know that. If they'd wanted me dead they'd have fired a hundred times, not three. Which means they weren't aiming for me – they were aiming for *you*.'

Hercufleas ground his teeth together. 'They're going to wish they *had* hit me,' he growled.

'Just *listen*,' Greta urged. 'On the count of three, I'll create a diversion. You jump over the walls. While they're looking out, you find a way in. The Black Death is in there somewhere. Get it, and get out. I'll meet you back here. But hurry – I won't be able to distract them for long!'

'But . . .'

'You know those shooting stars last night?' she said. 'You're like them. You're carrying all our hopes. You can't let them fizzle out. I don't want them to fizzle out. Are you ready?'

Hercufleas nodded. He crouched on her shoulder,

feeling the tension build in his legs.

'One . . .'

This was going to be the greatest jump of his life.

'Two . . .'

Or the last.

'Three!'

WHOOSH! Up, up he went, catapulting over the red-brick walls of the fortress, while Greta shrank beneath him. He saw her aim the rusted Howlitzer and fire. A wailing shriek flew from the barrel, and the shadowy figures on the fortress battlements ducked down, holding their ears.

Hercufleas landed in the corner of the courtyard. The first thing he noticed was that there were no more fortresses inside this one. Instead there was a stone chest, sealed shut. That was it: the Black Death – the only weapon capable of destroying Yuk – was within reach.

He was about to hop towards it when he noticed the creatures guarding the fortress. They scurried over the battlements, peered out of the towers and barricaded the portcullis, aiming tiny cannons at Greta . . .

They were everywhere.

The whole fortress was infested with dirty brown mice.

And a column of them marched straight towards him.

27

The mice carried gleaming muskets the size of pencils, filled with saltpetre and shot, and wore faded uniforms of burgundy, gold and zaffre. They had high leather boots, and floppy hats with budgie feathers in them. At the head of the column was an old albino mouse, with fierce red eyes and pure white fur and a slender silver sword in his paw.

It was too late to hide – they'd spotted Hercufleas the moment he landed. There was nothing he could do except stand and wait.

'I am Sir Klaus,' the albino mouse said, 'the smallest hero in Petrossia! These,' he gestured behind him, 'are my Mousketeers.'

'All for one, and one for all!' the Mousketeers cheered.

'And this,' said Sir Klaus, sword pointing straight at Hercufleas, 'is Grimm.'

Hercufleas looked cross-eyed at the blade's needle point.

'Hello, Grimm,' he said. 'Can you tell your master to stop shooting his guns at the girl outside? He says he's a hero, but it doesn't seem very heroic to *me* to shoot an innocent human child.'

Sir Klaus narrowed his blazing red eyes, but raised his left paw and called, 'Cease!' The *pop-pop-pop* of tiny cannons fell silent.

'No one that seeks the Black Death is innocent,' Sir Klaus said. 'Especially not a child travelling with a *flea*. You have come for the plague, have you not?'

Hercufleas nodded. 'Yes.'

There were mutterings from the mice around the fortress. Sir Klaus's pink tail went rigid with fury.

'Then you would unleash it upon the Earth a second time! We are sworn to stop you!'

'I only want to bite one creature, that's all,' Hercufleas insisted. 'He's a giant called Yuk. . .'

Sir Klaus laughed. 'The Black Death won't end its killing with *one death*. It will spread. Millions of victims are not enough to satisfy it.'

Hercufleas looked around in dismay. 'But listen, it's for the good of—'

'No good can come from the Black Death, only evil.' Sir Klaus raised his sword. 'Die, you monster!'

Hercufleas bounded back from the weapon. 'I'm not a monster, I'm a hero!' he said indignantly.

'Lies!' cried Sir Klaus. 'We Mousketeers are the heroes, sworn to protect Petrossia and the world! You are a villainous evil-doer!'

'No, *I'm* trying to save the world too!' shrieked Hercufleas. 'You're the villains – shooting children, poking swords at defenceless bugs.'

Sir Klaus's ears twitched, eyes burning with rage. Grimm snagged in the air, mid-swipe. 'What did you just say?'

'How do we know *you're* the heroes?' answered Hercufleas, raising his voice to talk to the Mousketeers in the fortress around him. 'In my experience, it's easy to mistake the two. I've come here for the Black Death, but to save lives, not destroy them. Maybe *I'm* the hero. We can't *both* be right, can we? Shouldn't we have a duel or something, to decide?'

Sir Klaus looked at his Mousketeers, who were

frowning and nodding, and his tail whipped the ground. He whirled on his heel with an irritated huff. 'Agreed!' he snapped, marching to the far side of the courtyard. 'A duel it shall be: you versus me.'

Hercufleas gulped and nodded, but Sir Klaus was three times his size, and his sword was long and deadly. What chance did he have? He was utterly terrified, but he knew he could not let his fear show. So he grinned and picked up a grain of sand to sharpen his tiny fangs on, and in Sir Klaus's red eyes he saw a flicker of fear.

'Very well,' Hercufleas called. 'If my blood is spilled, then I'm clearly not the hero, for heroes never lose. You may squash me under your paw.'

Sir Klaus smiled thinly. 'I shall.'

'But,' continued Hercufleas, and as he spoke he began to hop in excitement, for in his head he felt the whirrings and stirrings of a plan. 'If *I* win, then I *am* the hero, and you must swear to give me the Black Death I need.'

The Mousketeers looked at each other in bewilderment and anger.

'Give up the plague we have sworn to protect?' snarled Sir Klaus. 'To a flea, of all creatures? Ha!'

'Fine,' said Hercufleas with a shrug. 'Then you are a coward that refuses to fight me, afraid that you are wrong . . .'

Sir Klaus's whiskers twitched. 'Never!' he bellowed. 'It is agreed! I will fight this flea. Mousketeers, you will stand and witness our battle. Watch for the first drop of blood that is spilled. Let the duel begin!'

28

Sir Klaus leaped forward, blade whirling, forcing Hercufleas back against the fortress walls. Raising Grimm, the mouse raked his sword against the red bricks. Grimm's tip snapped off, and sparks leaped from the steel. Blinded, Hercufleas hopped behind Sir Klaus, smacking straight into the knight's tail.

The Mousketeers cheered as Hercufleas lay dazed on the tail's tip. His head was reeling, but so far everything was going to plan.

Come on, he thought, while Sir Klaus grinned and high-pawed his soldiers. *Come on . . .*

'Dizzy, Hercufleas?' laughed the mouse as Hercufleas clung to his tail. 'I must admit, I did not think you would surrender so easily . . .'

Hercufleas said nothing. He crouched, ready to jump.

Come on, he thought again, willing the mouse to strike. *Come on!*

And Sir Klaus raised his sword.

Yes! He's fallen for it!

When Sir Klaus struck, Hercufleas would leap clear of the blade. The mouse would slice the tip from his tail, spilling his own blood, and defeat himself.

'Die!' cried Sir Klaus.

Hercufleas jumped.

But something was wrong. Sir Klaus was swinging too high! The sword wasn't heading for where Hercufleas had been – it was slicing towards where he was going!

Sir Klaus had seen through the trick.

He's outwitted me! I'm jumping straight into Grimm's path! I'll be chopped in half!

Somersaulting in the air, Hercufleas reacted on impulse as the blade sliced towards him. Everything slowed down in his mind. He saw Grimm's razor-sharp edge, and at the last moment he kicked his legs sideways. His feet hit the edge of the sword, deflecting it an inch upward. It glided harmlessly above him. Just.

Sir Klaus hissed in annoyance and cracked his tail like a whip. It struck Hercufleas and catapulted him into the floor – *oomph* – where he skidded among the pebbles and frost.

What should he do now?

'You say you are a hero?' Sir Klaus paced back and forth, waiting for him to get up. 'Yet you use sly tricks more worthy of a knave!'

Hercufleas had no time to answer before Sir Klaus launched another deadly attack. Left and right, high and low, Grimm stabbed and swept and slashed and hacked and spun. Hercufleas hopped back, retreating, desperately trying to think of a new plan. He needed one quickly. Already he was exhausted. But so was Sir Klaus.

Sweat dripped from the old mouse's whiskers as he pursued the flea up a tower staircase, across the fortress walls, down a turret roof, trying to land a killing blow.

The Mousketeers looked on in awe. Never before had they seen such stunning swordsmanship, or such amazing acrobatics. It was like a dance – a grim fandango – and everyone could see that it could not go on for much longer.

Hercufleas tumbled back down into the courtyard. He lay there, while Sir Klaus descended the turret steps slowly, panting.

'I do declare,' he said, 'you have entirely exhausted my right paw. I have not had to fight left-pawed since defending my cousins the rats in Hamelin.'

As Sir Klaus switched his sword from right paw to left, Hercufleas's mind raced. He was running out of time.

Then he saw it.

His only hope.

Hercufleas jumped –

Sir Klaus glanced up –

'Where did he go?' blinked the mouse, whirling round.

On all sides of the castle, the Mousketeers gasped. In torment they watched their champion turn left and right, looking for his enemy. Each one yearned to tell Sir Klaus where Hercufleas was, but this was a duel and they were honour-bound not to interfere.

Clinging to Sir Klaus's back, Hercufleas was utterly still. He wouldn't be able to hold on for much longer. It didn't matter. His fangs, slender as syringe needles, sank into his enemy's fur and drained a thimble of blood.

Sir Klaus felt his shoulder itch. He squeaked and stabbed backwards, but his broken sword couldn't reach. If he swung too recklessly, he could injure himself and lose the duel. Finally his tail wrapped around Hercufleas like a python and whipped the flea round to face the mouse's ferocious stare.

'You fought well,' he said, in the absolute silence of the courtyard. 'But you have lost this duel, and therefore your life. Die, monster.'

And with the jagged edge of Grimm, Sir Klaus stabbed Hercufleas in the belly.

Pain skewered him. His armoured skin crunched as a fat drop of blood welled out from his swollen stomach.

'It is over. You will never have the Black Death.'

But Hercufleas, though he was slick and red with blood, gave a weak laugh.

And Sir Klaus knew what he had done.

'*NO!*' he cried, but it was too late. The drop of blood splished onto the courtyard floor.

'You spilled your own blood.' Hercufleas laughed, though laughing hurt. 'The blood inside me is the blood I drank from you just now. I win. I win!'

A groan went up from the Mousketeers. It was true. They'd seen it happen. Sir Klaus looked at them, then back at Hercufleas in his grasp. Then he dropped the broken sword to the floor and fell on his knees, squeaking and sobbing.

'I have lost,' wept Sir Klaus. 'Forgive me, world, for failing to protect you. The Black Death must be unleashed again.'

Hercufleas lay on the ground in agony, his broken body grating against itself with each breath. He had won the duel, but at what cost? Everything seemed suddenly far away. Sir Klaus came close but Hercufleas could barely see him. What was the mouse saying? Why was it so cold? When had it got so dark?

29

Hercufleas woke on a mouse-hair mattress. For a brief, wonderful moment, he thought he was back in the house-hat and everything had been a long, detailed and extremely far-fetched dream. He sat up, looking for Min and Pin; then the pain in his belly made him double over.

He remembered: the fortress, the duel, the drop of blood . . .

He collapsed back down on the bed, gasping, wondering how he was still alive. Gingerly he prodded his tummy. The wound was sealed with candle wax and stitched shut with mouse whiskers. The Mousketeers had saved his life!

How long had he slept? He was ravenous. By his bedside was a tiny goblet with a drop of mouse blood in it. He gulped it down (suppressing the desire to nibble cheese) and looked around the room. It was cylindrical and made of red brick. He was still in the fortress, then, in one of the turrets. A young sandy-haired Mousketeer with an azure uniform dozed on guard duty by the door. When Hercufleas plonked the goblet down, he gave a squeak, clutched at his musket and saluted.

'You're awake!' Opening the door, he called, 'Sir Klaus!'

Footsteps pattered up the spiral stairs.

'You have recovered,' the albino mouse said stiffly, coming into the room. 'Then it is time.'

'Time?' Hercufleas didn't understand. 'For what?'

The old mouse stroked his white whiskers. 'For me to keep my vow. You won our duel. Every Mousketeer before me has pledged never to let the Black Death out into the world again. Yet I promised to obey you, though I do so with a heavy heart.'

Hercufleas bounced upright. 'You're really giving me the Black Death?'

Sir Klaus grimaced. 'No,' he said. 'I'm giving you a choice. There is a difference. The Black Death is a weapon. You must choose to wield it, or leave it be.'

Hercufleas nodded, remembering the empty houses of Tumber. Greta's broken heart. His missing fleamily.

Sir Klaus might think he was giving him a choice, but what choice did he have?

'I will wield it,' he said at last.

Sir Klaus looked at the sandy-haired mouse, who saluted and closed the door behind him. He sat in a chair beside the bed. Suddenly he looked very old.

'I need it,' Hercufleas said, trying to make Sir Klaus understand. He thought back to what Miss Witz had told him. 'Arthur had Excalibur. Roland had Durendal. The Black Death is my weapon. I need it to be a hero. Otherwise there won't be a Happily Ever After.'

'Happily Ever Afters do not come from weapons,' Sir Klaus said wearily. 'Weapons are not an ending, they are the beginning of a cycle. First death. Then from death comes heartbreak, and from heartbreak comes hate, and the white heat of hate forges more weapons.'

'What else can I do, Sir Klaus? This is the only way to defeat Yuk.'

'There is always another way. You just have to believe.'

Hercufleas shook his head. 'Believing isn't enough.'

'Believing is more than you think.' Klaus blinked his red eyes. 'To survive, you must believe in something greater than you. Just like your kind, who live off bigger animals. We are all fleas on the back of a creature called

Hope. What about the girl who came with you to this place?'

Hercufleas smiled sadly. 'Greta doesn't believe in anything.'

'She believes in you.' Klaus stood up and went to the window. 'Why else is she still here?'

Hercufleas leaped out of bed, this time ignoring the pain. 'Greta?' He wobbled over to the window, looking out across the courtyard where he and Sir Klaus had fought their duel. There she was, sitting on the battlements, clogs swinging, green scarf streaming in the wind. She was chatting with the Mousketeers while they climbed over Artifax. Hercufleas smiled. He had missed her odd-eyed stares and rare-as-dodo-blood smiles.

'I thought she'd give up,' Hercufleas said, swaying on his feet. 'Go back to Tumber.'

Klaus rested his paw on Hercufleas's shoulder to steady him. 'She stayed here. Four days it has been. Because she thinks you can defeat Yuk.'

Hercufleas felt himself flush pink. 'You mean she thinks the *Black Death* can defeat Yuk.'

Klaus laughed. 'I do not think so. She does not speak of the Black Death. She speaks of you and your heroic deeds – like firing yourself from a pig's snout, and being swallowed by a fish.'

Hercufleas stared down at Greta from the window and saw hope in her face, fragile and fierce as a sparrow. But hope for what?

'You must make the right choice,' said Sir Klaus gravely. 'Do you put your trust in the power of death? Or will you trust in another power: yourself?'

30

When Greta saw Hercufleas, she ran across the courtyard in a cloud of dust and scattered mice. She pressed her eye to the window to gaze at him, soaking the sill with her tears.

'You're awake!' Her voice boomed around the room, making Hercufleas's head ring. 'I knew you'd be fine, I knew it! You did it, Hercufleas! They're going to give us the Black Death!'

Hercufleas didn't know what to say. He looked at Sir Klaus. Was the mouse right? Could he really defeat Yuk without such a dreadful weapon? How could he trust in himself when he had failed so many times already?

'Come,' said Sir Klaus, leading Hercufleas down the spiral stairs. Outside it was evening, and the granite chest threw a long tombstone shadow across the courtyard.

Two Mousketeers were busy unsealing the keyhole above the lid.

'You alone can gather the Black Death,' Sir Klaus said, stooped and hollow-eyed. 'Go in through the keyhole and take a sip of the plague. But know this: it cannot be undone. You will carry the Black Death for the rest of your life. Anyone you bite will die. And once you unleash the plague upon the world, there is no telling where it might spread. Whom it might destroy.'

Greta turned pale and looked down at Hercufleas.

'Are you ready?' she asked.

Do you want to back out? is what she meant.

'Yes,' he said, jumping through the keyhole, unsure which question he was answering.

It was dark inside the chest. Still. Lifeless as a crypt. Nothing moved but the dust dancing in the sunbeam that slanted in through the keyhole and down onto a lead-lined box. Hercufleas hopped closer, stale air swirling around him, blood churning in his belly. The sunbeam was hot on his back, but the lid when he touched it was cold. It sucked the warmth from his fingers. In his head, the words of Sir Klaus and Miss Witz clashed together.

No good can come of the Black Death, only evil.

I wish there was another way.

Make the right choice.

Save us.

He heaved the lid up. The lead seal broke and a rancid smell rushed up, like a ghost flying free from its coffin. Inside the box was the glass phial, just as Miss Witz had described. It was filled with water and a single black speck, like a dried inkblot.

The Black Death.

Hard to believe that something so small could be so deadly.

Hercufleas could scarcely breathe. He grasped the phial. All he had to do was pull out the stopper and swallow the plague. Then he'd have the power to save his fleamily. To protect Tumber. To avenge Greta.

Inside the glass, the tiny black speck shifted. It *moved*. He'd woken the Black Death. It could sense him. And he could feel it too. It hungered for life. It had to take life to live.

Min's voice came to him then: *Be careful, Hercufleas. You are what you eat.*

He shoved the phial back into the box and slammed the lid shut.

He couldn't. Mustn't. Eating something so monstrous would make a monster of him. With one leap he bounded back towards the light. In the dark he thought he heard a howl of rage – or was that just the wind whistling through the keyhole?

Suddenly he was back in the courtyard, gasping. He gazed up at the expectant faces.

'Hercufleas?' It was Greta. 'Do you have it? You were gone for ages. What happened in there?'

He couldn't tell her he'd let her down again. So he looked at Sir Klaus. 'I made a choice,' he said, and nodded.

The mouse slumped with relief, his red eyes filling with tears. He turned to Greta. 'Trust in this flea,' he said. 'He is a great hero. Believe in him, and he will never fail you.'

Greta smiled. 'Of course he won't! He's Hercufleas, the most unbe*flea*vably powerful parasite in the world! Now he can destroy Yuk with a single bite!'

She thought he had the Black Death. Of course she did. Why wouldn't she? Hercufleas couldn't meet her eyes. Freezing in the tundra, getting swallowed by a fish, duelling a mouse . . . It had all been for nothing, because he couldn't bring the Black Death back into the world. Now he risked everything he cared about.

His fleamily.

The Tumberfolk.

And perhaps more important and fragile than any of those things: Greta's smile.

The Mousketeers loaded Artifax with supplies before they left: tiny waxed wheels of cheese, seeds and salted meat, and an enormous blanket stitched together from hundreds of their spare quilts, to keep out the cold.

When the time came, Sir Klaus assembled his troops in the courtyard. The worry had fallen away from him, now he knew the Black Death was still in its chest. The old mouse looked young again.

'Before you go,' he called, 'I have a gift for Hercufleas! Bring it here!'

The sandy-haired Mousketeer from Hercufleas's room hurried across the courtyard, holding a plump scarlet cushion. On it was the shard from the tip of Grimm that had splintered off during the duel. It had been reforged and fitted with a minute handle.

'Go on,' Sir Klaus urged. 'It was made just for you.'

Gingerly, Hercufleas picked up the sword and swept

the blade left and right. It felt perfect in his grasp – like an extra fang.

'Every hero must go on a quest to find his weapon,' Klaus said, smiling.

'Thank you,' Hercufleas replied solemnly. 'I shall name it *m*, because it came from the end of your sword, *Grimm*. And the letter *m*, if you trace it in the air with your paw, makes the shape of a jumping flea.'

Sir Klaus laughed. 'I do believe that is the smallest name for a sword in all the world. Which is fitting, for it belongs to the smallest hero.'

Hercufleas nodded, trying his best to hide his fears. 'What will I do?' he murmured to Sir Klaus, too quietly for Greta's human ears. 'A splinter-sized sword won't be enough to defeat a giant.'

Sir Klaus stroked his whiskers, nodding. Then he leaned forward and gave Hercufleas a crushing hug. 'Trust me,' he whispered. 'When you reach Tumber, look in the faces of the people there. A way to defeat Yuk will appear, I promise you. Just look at the Tumberfolk, and you will see it.'

'What do you mean? What way?' But Klaus was squeezing him so tight the words came out in a croak. The Mousketeer put him back on the floor.

'Time to go,' said Greta, pointing at the sun melting on the horizon. As they watched, it dripped below the earth and sputtered out like a candle. Night fell quickly up in the Waste, and they had to get back to Tumber before Yuk came.

Hercufleas gulped. He wanted to ask Sir Klaus more questions, but there wasn't time. Before he could open his mouth, Greta scooped him up and leaped on Artifax.

Out from the red-brick fortress they went, while the Mousketeers lined the walls and played a fanfare on tiny brass bugles.

'Three cheers for the Mousketeers!' they cried. 'But Hercufleas is the bee's knees! And Greta is even better!'

Greta laughed, waving goodbye. She took the Howlitzer, which the mice had helped her scrub free of rust, loading it with her own goodbye. She fired it into the air, so loud it made the whole fortress shake.

'And Sir Klaus is the world's greatest mouse!'

Off they rode, heading for Tumber. It would be a close thing. The half-moon shone above them. They had journeyed twelve days, then stayed with the mice for another four. In just under a fortnight, when the moon was new and the night was darkest, Yuk would return.

'We *will* make it.' She grinned at Hercufleas, hopping anxiously on her shoulder. 'We've got food, and protection from the cold, and I know the way now.'

Hercufleas forced a smile. Two weeks to find a new way to defeat Yuk – one that didn't involve the Black Death. He counted in his head what he and Greta were bringing back from their quest:

1. A splinter-sized sword.

2. A gun that fired noise.

3. A week's supply of cheese.

That was it. It didn't seem much. Not anywhere near enough. *A way to defeat Yuk will appear*, Sir Klaus had promised. *Just look at the Tumberfolk.* He tried to make himself believe it.

Artifax ran on, faster than a cheetah, racing through the many layers of the Czar's fortress. Then they were out on the Waste again, wind howling, frost crunching underfoot.

Towards Tumber.

Towards Yuk.

Towards a battle Hercufleas did not know how to win.

31

The journey back was different. Now it was Hercufleas who sat moody and silent, while Greta talked about her family from dawn to gloaming. She told him of evenings spent eating plumpkin pies, drinking nettle tea and listening to Papa's stories in the warm treacly light of the tinderfly lamp. Days when Mama came back late from the woodn't and hugged Greta tight, her coat thick with the smell of pine needles. And Wuff, with his scruffy fur and floppy ears. How he used to sit, paws crossed, by the stove. She told Hercufleas things she hadn't let herself remember for a long time, fearing they would be too painful.

Then Greta found she wanted to talk about the future too. About how life would be when Yuk was gone.

'I'll build a new home from everpines and invite the

Mousketeers to stay . . . I'll brew nettle tea, and it'll always taste sweet . . . I'm going to find where the green giants sleep and wake them up.'

That roused Hercufleas from his gloomy thoughts. 'Haven't you had enough of giants?'

She laughed. 'Not all of them are like Yuk, you know.'

And that night by the fire, huddled under the blanket, Greta explained: 'Papa told me about the green giants. Before them, all Petrossia was like it is out here on the Waste. Then they came along, planting the forests and bringing life.' She made her voice deep and dreamy: '*Long ago, back in the time when trees could speak and laugh and rhyme, green giants walked among the firs, like Mother Nature's gardeners.*'

Hercufleas was sleepy. 'What happened to them?' he yawned, cuddling up in her scarf.

Greta shrugged. 'They fell asleep. No one knows where. Just think . . . somewhere out there, so deep in the forest that the trees still whisper to each other, there are these enormous people. Big as cathedrals. All sleeping on beds of wildflowers.'

'Wish we could wake them,' Hercufleas mumbled. 'There'd be no more woodn'ts, only woods. No more rattlesnoaks. No more pine-needlers. No more Yuk either.'

Greta smiled. 'We don't need green giants for that,' she said, burying her chin in her scarf. 'We've got you.'

Hercufleas went quiet. Ever since leaving the fortress, he had fixed a confident smile upon his face and never let it slip. It was like wearing a mask. And if Greta saw behind it, she would know the truth.

'How will you do it?' she asked him, the next night.

'Do what?'

'Give Yuk the Black Death,' Greta said. She took a wheel of cheese from their supplies, speared it on a stick and began toasting it over the flames. 'Do you just have to bite him somewhere? Or does it have to be a weak spot? And then what happens next? How long until he drops down dead? Will he swell up and go pop? Do his eyes fall out? Will his insides turn to mush?'

'I don't know,' Hercufleas said, trying to hide his discomfort.

Greta's eyes burned as she stared at the flames. 'Hope it hurts,' she whispered.

Hercufleas shuddered. Greta took the bubbling cheese from the embers, sliced off the soft wax and dipped some roots she had gathered in the gooey centre. Artifax clucked as he gulped them down. Greta smiled and scratched his neck while he ate. Then she pricked her thumb again and gave Hercufleas a thimble of her blood – it was the sweetest and coolest he had ever tasted it, with another flavour too, dark and breathless.

It was anticipation. Greta couldn't wait to destroy Yuk. To finally get her revenge.

'Hey,' she said, looking up. 'What's that?'

Hercufleas followed her gaze. Down from the dark sky a white and silent speck fell towards them. It settled by the fire, like the ghost of a tinderfly come to spark itself back to life.

Another flake came down, out of the breathless cold. Then dozens, hundreds, uncountable thousands. Artifax stared in confusion. Cautiously he pecked a few from his wing.

'What are they?' whispered Hercufleas.

Greta looked up at the clouds. 'Miss Witz told us about this in school,' she whispered back. 'I think it's snow.'

'Snow,' breathed Hercufleas. Then he said, 'Why are we whispering?'

Greta opened her mouth, then shrugged. It was as if something wonderful was coming close and if they talked too loud, they might frighten it off.

She stood up, peering into the night around them, Hercufleas in her palm.

'Miss Witz said, if you see snow, it means the Snow Merchant is close.'

And, her voice a murmur, she told him the legend. Of a silver-haired old woman who travelled the world with a stone bird upon her shoulder, bringing snow wherever she went, working a sort of alchemy upon winter: changing it from something ugly into something beautiful. And whoever gave her a place to stay, she signed her name as 'Snow Merchant' in blue ink upon their ledger. But why she walked, and where she came from, and where she was going, the legend didn't say. Greta's breath caught in her throat. 'There!'

Upon the faraway hills Hercufleas saw a tiny flickering light as someone with a lantern made their lonely way across the Waste.

'Is that the Snow Merchant?' whispered Hercufleas. 'Is the legend true?'

Greta smiled her fragile smile, that grew stronger and fiercer with each day, and said quietly, 'I don't know. But I believe.'

Next day Artifax took them across a pure white landscape, glittering and silent. The Waste was still desolate and cold, but the Snow Merchant had made it magical too.

Hercufleas thought a lot about that. Believing was not a weapon, but it had a quiet power nonetheless. He might not be bringing the Black Death back to Tumber, but Greta was bringing back her belief. Perhaps that would be enough. It had to be.

32

Past the Sorrows and through the woodn't they went, miles and days rushing past.

Twelve nights later, an exhausted Artifax reached Tumber at sunset. Greta rode him across the bridge, stopping to take two sips of water from the banks of the river.

'Taking my tears back,' she said.

Up ahead, the town was dark and silent.

'*HEY!*' called Greta. '*HEEEY! WE'RE BACK!*'

A light winked on by the bridge, and Mrs Lorrenz pulled up her sash window. Her fat face was smeared with cream cheese and she had pink macaroons on her eyes.

'Who is shouting?' she bellowed. 'Stop interrupting my beauty sleep! If I'm going to be guzzled, I want to look my best!'

'It's Greta, Mrs Lorrenz! And I've brought the mightiest hero in all the world to save us!'

Mrs Lorrenz pulled the macaroons from her eyes. 'Who?'

The Tumberfolk were emerging from their homes now, timid as hedgehogs, for the new moon was tonight and Yuk would return in a few hours.

Mayor Klare came bobbing down the road, golden key jangling around his neck. 'The mightiest hero?' he said. 'Do you mean Teresa the Weightless, the greatest alchemist ever to have lived?'

'No, she must mean Peter!' said Mrs Lorrenz. 'Petrossia's last genius!'

'Oh.' Mayor Klare stopped a few paces from Artifax. 'It's just that woodlouse thing.'

With one stubby finger, Mrs Lorrenz wiped up a blob of cream cheese that had fallen off her nose and popped it in her mouth. 'That woodlouse is no hero. He said it himself! We're still doomed!'

'And it's *still* all Greta's fault!' sniped Mayor Klare, flicking through his ledger. 'Surely it has to be a crime to fill a town with false hope. Ah, yes, it is – it says so here.'

Hercufleas looked around at the Tumberfolk. There wasn't anything in their faces that would help him fight

Yuk. What had Sir Klaus meant? All he saw was hope snuffed out, leaving black despair. They didn't believe in him like Greta did.

'Quick, let me load up the Howlitzer,' he murmured.

'For the crime of making false promises,' Mayor Klare read from his ledger, 'I do hereby sentence Greta to wear an overturned fish bowl on her head, so no one else need hear her lies!'

'Whatever size his enemies, the winner's always Hercufleas!'

The Howlitzer blew Mayor Klare off his feet. It made Mrs Lorrenz's windowpanes explode. The whole town reeled at the power of it.

'It's Yuk!' shrieked the mayor. 'He's here! By the power vested in me, I do hereby declare that everyone should run around like headless chickens!'

He raced off with his cloak over his head, collided with a wall and sprawled across the cobbles, out cold.

'Now,' said Hercufleas to the Tumberfolk, 'are you going to take me seriously, or do I need to repeat myself?'

'He *is* a hero,' Greta called to them. 'Just listen to everything that he's done!'

And she told the crowd of their quest through the

woodn't, beyond the Sorrows, into the frozen Waste and the heart of the Czar's ruined fortress, where Hercufleas had found the world's deadliest weapon. The Tumberfolk were spellbound as Greta told them of the tiny hero with his shining splinter of a sword. They gasped when she spoke the words *Black Death*, and gradually they all began to chant:

'Whatever size his enemies, the winner's always Hercufleas!'

'Listen to me,' Hercufleas cried. 'Yuk is coming this very night!'

'What do we do?' asked a cinderwikk man nervously. 'The mayor should tell us.'

'I think we should—' began a cossack.

'Why don't we—'a roost-wife interrupted.

'How about—'

'Perhaps—'

'Quiet!' called Hercufleas, but already the whole town was arguing among themselves and he could not be heard.

He spotted the black robes and golden key, lying beside the unconscious Mayor Klare. Leaping over to them, Hercufleas began to swing the key on its ribbon. It took nearly all his strength, but he whirled around, faster and faster, and finally let go.

Up into the air the key flew, over the heads of the bickering crowd. Everyone turned to see it land around the neck of Miss Witz, who was hobbling up the road towards them.

The arguments stopped at once. Everyone gawped at the old babushka. She raised her charcoal eyebrows at the key, then fixed everyone with her steely gaze that had made so many of the Tumberfolk tremble when they were five years old.

It had the same effect now.

'Follow my instructions exactly,' she announced. 'Greta has brought us our hero. Hercufleas carries the weapon. Now we must get ready.'

'For what?' asked one of the bakers of Butterbröt Lane.

'For battle,' Mayor Witz answered. 'Isn't that right, Hercufleas?'

'The battle will be fierce.' He hopped forward. 'Our only hope . . .'

He trailed off. What was their only hope? Hercufleas racked his brain. Sir Klaus had told him he would find it when he reached Tumber again, but there was nothing here. Just anxious human faces, all staring at him . . .

And suddenly he knew. Sir Klaus was right. Of course there was hope. The answer had been here all along: the Tumberfolk.

'We must fight together,' he said.

And he knew that he was right, for everyone and everything – even Mayor Witz's copper bell – was silent.

The Tumberfolk exchanged wary looks.

'We've never had to fight before,' one of the roost-wives quibbled. 'The other heroes always told us to go home and hide.'

Hercufleas scowled. 'I'm not like other heroes,' he answered. 'I'm going to win. But I can't face Yuk on my own. No one can. He's too big. But look how many of us there are! Like cogs in a machine, like bits of a puzzle, like fleas in a swarm, we can join together to make something enormous, bigger even than a giant. Not you or me . . . but *us.*'

But the crowd murmured and fidgeted. The roost-wives looked mistrustfully at the cinderwikk men, and a cossack spat on the ground in the direction of the bakers of Butterbröt Lane. The Tumberfolk needed something more to believe in than just each other, but what else could Hercufleas tell them?

Greta blurted out the words: 'And while you fight together, Hercufleas will find Yuk's weak point, and bite down hard, and the Black Death will destroy Yuk from the inside out. Isn't that right, Hercufleas?'

Hercufleas watched Mayor Witz's copper bell from the corner of his eye. Greta had believed her words to be true, but if he spoke now, the lie would be revealed.

So he just nodded, as solemnly as he could. Telling the truth wasn't important. Pretending he had the Black Death would make Tumber believe. If he could do that, they might have a chance. Belief was a sort of glue. It held people together when terrible things tried to prise them apart.

'What do we fight with?' said someone at last.

'Excellent question,' said Mayor Witz, picking a stick

of chalk from her pocket and writing *WEAPONS* on the side of a house like it was a blackboard. 'Suggestions?'

'I have my axe,' said Greta, raising her hand. 'And the Howlitzer.'

'We have a thousand tinderflies,' said a cinderwikk man. 'On their own they aren't much, but lump them together . . .'

'Wonderful!' said Mayor Witz, chalking up the ideas. 'What else?'

The bakers of Butterbröt Lane held up their rolling pins. The cossacks showed their knives and snares and bows. Their huskies growled, baring their teeth. Artifax flexed his powerful feet and clacked sharp claws on the cobbles, and seeing him, the chickens on the heads of the roost-wives clucked menacingly.

Hercufleas smiled. The Tumberfolk were still scared, but now they were determined too. He had done it: he had made them believe.

'Greta?'

'What?' she murmured, while Mayor Witz organised everyone into attack formation.

'I've got a special mission for you,' he said. 'Only you can do it. While I'm finding Yuk's weak spot, I want you to rescue my fleamily. They're trapped on Yuk's head, in

196

the branches of that rattlesnoak. If I . . . If something goes wrong, will you try to save them?'

She frowned. 'Nothing's going to go wrong. Not now you've got the power of the Black Death in you.'

'I know, but . . .' He tried to keep the doubt from his voice. 'Will you promise me anyway? I know you keep your promises.'

She looked at him with her odd eyes. 'All right,' she said. 'I promise.'

33

As night drew on, Tumber prepared. The cinderwikk men stuffed every tinderfly they had into a barrel and rolled it to the ruined church of Saint Katerina on the Hill. That was where Mayor Witz had decided the battle should be fought. The Tumberfolk repaired the church roof as best as they could, then painted sloppy white letters across the tiles:

OPEN ME

No one knew whether or not Yuk could read, but he was sure to be attracted to the huge sign. He'd stomp up the hill, tear off the roof . . . and fall right into the trap.

Inside, everyone gathered. The bakers of Butterbröt Lane hefted their rolling pins. The roost-wives sharpened the beaks of their hens. Only the cossacks were missing:

Mayor Witz had stationed them by the river to prepare nets and snares.

In a corner, Greta checked her Howlitzer. She had filled it with shouts and screams. Everything Yuk had made her suffer, she poured back into the barrel, to shoot straight back at him.

Slowly, steadily, time ticked on towards midnight. The Tumberfolk settled down to wait. They crossed their fingers and prayed at the shrine of Saint Clover, patron saint of luck. Hercufleas prayed too, but only on the inside. On the outside he wore a fierce and determined smile. He hopped from person to person, joking, listening and calming their fears. When hope was all you had to fight with, doubt was the deadliest enemy of all.

DONG went the first chime of midnight.

Everyone in the church froze, listening. This was the time. The moon was new, the night was darkest and Yuk was coming. They trembled as the rest of the chimes faded away to silence.

Then they heard his footsteps.

Big footsteps.

Enormous footsteps.

From feet that could splash through lakes as if they were puddles, and kick the tops off mountains.

Coming closer.

Yuk strode into the town. He kicked over houses like a bully kicks sandcastles, heading for the church on the hill. His stomach was rumbling with hunger. Hercufleas was so frightened that a small brown scab dropped onto the floor behind him.

The Tumberfolk quivered and shook. They were like autumn leaves barely clinging to a tree branch, and Yuk was like a gale of wind coming to tear them from their stems.

'This is hopeless,' whispered the cinderwikk men.

'Madness!' whimpered the roost-wives.

Even Mayor Witz's resolve had melted away. 'I'm too old to die!'

For a moment it seemed as if everyone might throw down their weapons and run away screaming. Then a tiny, soothing voice sounded in each of their ears, telling them what they needed to hear – giving them a reason to fight.

'For the children!' it whispered to Mayor Witz.

'For your parents!' it whispered to Greta.

Hercufleas hopped about, pouring courage into everyone's ears, and at last the Tumberfolk lifted their weapons again.

'Battle stations!' Mayor Witz called.

THUMP,

    THUMP,

        THUMP, went the footsteps outside.

At once there was a wrenching, splintering crack. Timber and tiles fell from the ceiling, and the statue of Saint Clover toppled and smashed on the flagstones. Hercufleas squinted up past clouds of dust. The roof was gone. In its place was a long strip of stars. Yuk had ripped off the top of the church, exactly as planned.

'YUM.'

Leaning down, he stuck his whole face inside the church, like a pig in a trough. His rotten breath blasted in their faces, but the Tumberfolk stood firm. Hercufleas saw the worms burrowing through his teeth, the leeches swimming in his eyeballs. Rattleroots slithering in the roots of his hair . . .

And the house-hat! There it was! Still hanging from the branches of the tree sprouting from the giant's head. Filthy and upside down, but intact.

'Greta, fire!' he cried.

The Howlitzer shook in her grasp. She was paralysed with fear, or maybe hate.

'Fire! Now!'

201

Jumping, he barged her hesitating finger
aside and kicked the trigger with all his
might.

Out flew Greta's scream.

34

Never before or since has there been such a scream. All Greta's rage, pain, hate and sorrow shot from the barrel of the Howlitzer. Every grief, every hurt in her heart, blasted straight into Yuk's face.

Greta's scream gave the giant the fright of his life. He stepped back and tripped, rolling down the hill, flattening a dozen houses. The scream echoed around Tumber, making all the huskies howl and turning all the trees that lined the river to weeping willows. Then it was gone, and Greta collapsed to the floor, looking empty and faint.

The Tumberfolk cheered. For the first time, they saw Yuk was vulnerable.

'Focus!' Hercufleas told them. 'Ready the tinderflies!'

As Yuk staggered to his feet, the cinderwikk men rolled their barrel in place and put on their mirror-tinted goggles. The bakers from Butterbröt Lane whacked at the tin barrel with their rolling pins, driving the tinderflies inside into a furious frenzy. The metal turned black, then red, then white hot.

'Step back!' cried the cinderwikk men.

Roaring with anger, the giant stomped back up the hill. 'YUK WANTS TO GUZZLE!'

He thrust his head inside the church for a second time. The barrel exploded in his face.

It was like the sun had decided to rise early: a blinding fireball of tinderflies hit Yuk right on his chin, bursting apart into a million yellow and violet stars.

The giant's scream cracked the bell in the belfry and sent stained glass cascading down from the church windows. He reared back, but not fast enough. Before the tinderflies scattered on the wind, they brushed against his scratty beard of vines, setting it alight. Tumberfolk cheered as Yuk clawed at the flames on his chin, then turned and ran for the river.

He never saw the tripwire.

The cossacks pulled the rope taut across the street. It sent Yuk sprawling. He flew through the air like a flaming comet, then hit the ground. He crawled to the riverbank, dunking his beard in the water with a sizzling sound.

He whimpered with relief, letting the icy cold water soothe his charred chin. But when he tried to get up, he found he couldn't move.

The cossacks had thrown their iron nets over the giant. In seconds, they fixed them into the ground with stakes and hammers. Yuk strained against the cords – they tangled and snapped – the cossacks heaved and repegged – and the nets held firm.

Upon the hill, the Tumberfolk gawped at the giant in amazement. Now they realised their own power. Working together, they were mightier than any single hero could possibly be.

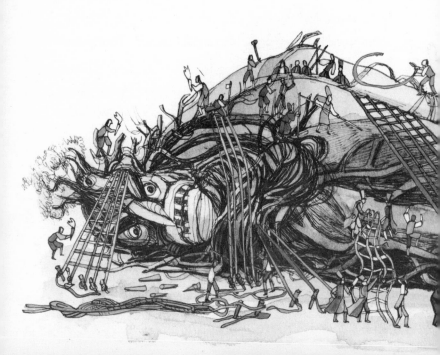

'Attack!' Hercufleas yelled, drawing *m*.

Everyone charged down the hill – a throng of bread-bakers and cake-makers and babushkas and roost-wives and chickens. Snared in the nets, Yuk was defenceless. The Tumberfolk swarmed over his back, thumping and whacking and jabbing. He thrashed about behind him, swatting with his one free hand, but his body was so full of caves and crags, the Tumberfolk just wriggled out of the way. The cinderwikk men started fires in his bellybutton. The huskies were chewing between his toes. Mayor Witz cackled as she flicked out the switchblade on her walking stick and jabbed it into his armpit.

'Chickens away!' screamed the roost-wives, pulling the bows on their heads and letting their cages of hair collapse. Dozens of furious hens flew squawking towards Yuk, pecking, scratching, screaming out 'BU-CAW!!'

And wherever you looked, there was Hercufleas, urging everyone on. He was a blur across the battle, on everyone's shoulder at once.

'Keep going!'

'Attack!'

'For Tumber!'

Realising he was beaten, the giant tried to retreat. He wrenched free of the last few nets and staggered to his feet. With a mighty kick, Artifax gouged Yuk's heel and he stumbled sideways. His foot snagged under the bridge called Two Tears, and the giant tripped. Hercufleas's stomach lurched – he thrust m into Yuk's skin to stop himself toppling off, but the blade came free and suddenly he was falling, falling . . .

With a thunderclap sound, the giant fell headfirst into the river.

Suddenly the tide of battle turned. The Tumberfolk swept off Yuk and into the water and came up spluttering. Their weapons sank to the riverbed. The hens bobbed downstream, out of reach.

Yuk looked down at the people floating in the river. Now they were the helpless ones.

'YUM,' he grinned. 'SOUP.'

Below him, the Tumberfolk splashed and floundered, praying to Saint Duffy, patron saint of mercy. Their courage was gone. They weren't an army any more – they were croutons, floating in Yuk's dinner.

'Help!' they cried. 'Hercufleas, save us! Bite Yuk now!'

But Hercufleas was nowhere to be seen.

Perhaps he had drowned in the river. Maybe he had run away. Whatever the truth, he was gone. No one could save the Tumberfolk now.

35

Yuk's nostril was a tunnel, fading into the distance. Bogeys sprouted like enormous mushrooms from all sides, glowing a fungal green. Stuck to them were skeletons of bats and birds who had flown inside by accident and become stuck. Hanging upside down, Hercufleas stared at the bones in despair.

So close. They'd been so close. He had tasted victory on his tongue, like the sweetest drop of blood. For a moment, he really had been a hero. Then something went wrong, and he'd found himself sliding into the cavern of Yuk's nose. Why did he always end up in nostrils?

He tried moving again. Kicked and squirmed and twisted. No good. His back was stuck on a piece of snot, sticky as treacle and smelly as over-boiled cabbage. It was no more than he deserved. Echoing around Yuk's nose were cries from outside. The Tumberfolk pleading with him to save them. He covered his ears with his hands. He couldn't bear to hear their shouts.

If only he had taken the Black Death.

If only . . .

A shadow passed over the far-off entrance. Something wriggled up the nostril towards him.

An enormous finger!

Hercufleas gasped. The disgusting brute was picking his nose!

He looked around the dim green glow of the bogeys for *m*. There! The sword glinted, just beyond his reach, embedded in the giant's nostril. *M* must be what was irritating him. Hercufleas strained to reach it. A little further. The finger wriggled up towards him, like an enormous worm. He gripped *m*'s hilt and pulled with the last of his strength.

The sword came out with a squelch. In two slices, Hercufleas was free. He dropped to the ground, the finger right behind him, and fled further up Yuk's nose. The nostril narrowed until it sloped sharply down. Foul air rushed overhead and there was a sound like enormous bellows wheezing. Where was he now?

'Aieeeeeeeeee!' A terrible scream echoed up from

somewhere below. Perched above Yuk's tonsils, Hercufleas saw a dim shape tumble down the giant's throat and vanish with a faraway *plop*.

'Mayor Klare!' he called out.

'Dooooooooooooooomed!' There was another high-pitched scream as Mrs Lorrenz followed him. She was so fat she got stuck halfway down. Yuk gulped, and she slid away into his stomach.

Hercufleas could not go down, only up. Drawing *m*, he pointed his sword above his head and prepared to jump. He crouched, eyes shut, legs shaking with tension, until at last he could hold it no more. Like a javelin, he pierced deep into Yuk's head. He couldn't breathe – something wet around him squelched and clenched and burst apart – then suddenly he gasped air and opened his eyes.

Where was he?

Greta was the only person left clinging to Yuk. Soaked, sodden, she watched from his shoulder as the giant wrenched a tree from the bank and used it like a broom to sweep all the Tumberfolk into the middle of the river. Then he snapped a tall chimney off the bakery on Butterbröt Lane and used it like a straw. He sucked up water and squirted it at the poor Tumberfolk. He blew bubbles under their feet and stirred them round and round.

'HA HA HA.'

Yuk was playing with his food before he ate it!

Then he began to guzzle.

First Mayor Klare, then Mrs Lorrenz . . . Greta watched in despair. She didn't know what had happened, only that Hercufleas was gone. Perhaps he had drowned. Or even abandoned them. She choked back a sob. She had believed in him. They all had.

Greta looked up. Yuk's head rose like the peak of a mountain. Suddenly she remembered the fleamily. She scowled. Tumber was doomed, but she could still save someone.

She tossed the Howlitzer down into the water. No need for it now. All she needed was her axe. She checked the edge. Keen. Slinging it over her shoulder, she began to climb.

36

Hercufleas thought Yuk's brain would be tiny – the size of a walnut maybe – but it was enormous. It looked like a spider's web – the most intricate, shimmering web that he had ever seen. White light pulsed along its threads, like a cityscape of interlocking streets and racing lantern-lit carriages.

Yuk's thoughts, he realised suddenly. *And the threads carry them around his head.*

It was dazzling and baffling at the same time. How could a creature that only cared about guzzling have a brain so complicated?

As he stood in awe, a little grey creature crawled quickly from a nexus of threads and looked nervously about. It was something between an octopus and a chimpanzee. It had eight legs, which it used to swing and jump from

214

thread to thread, as if they were branches in a forest, and only one eye.

Hercufleas ducked out of sight, gripping his sword tightly. As he watched, the creature spat out a new thread, like spaghetti from its mouth. Then it connected the thread to several others.

Hercufleas couldn't believe it. The octopanzee-thing – was it making the web of Yuk's brain even more complicated? Did that mean the giant was learning new things?

And if he could learn, could he change? Could he be taught that what he was doing to Tumber was wrong?

It was a staggering thought. Peering inside the giant's head, it was obvious that Yuk wasn't just a mindless monster that thought about nothing but his next meal. There was more going on here.

'*I beg your pardon, but are you a germ? A microbe or virus? A parasitic worm?*'

Hercufleas peered up to see the little octopanzee-thing dangling from a thread, talking to him. He'd been spotted! Now what?

'*Perhaps you're a plague? Or a fever of the head? Whatever you are – find another place to spread!*'

Hercufleas stared dumbly at the strange creature.

215

How could such a tiny part of Yuk's body be talking? How could it sound smarter than Yuk did? And why was it rhyming?

The creature squeaked in terror, and seven hands pointed behind Hercufleas. '*Whatever you are, you REALLY need to run – that rattleroot behind you is about to bite your bum!*'

Hercufleas whirled round. The rattleroot looked just like the shaft of Greta's axe, but was only the thickness of a cotton thread. It must be newly grown. A small head the size and colour and shape of a pumpkin seed had formed at the tip. While Hercufleas had been distracted by the strange sights of Yuk's brain, it had slithered up behind him. Now it bared its fangs.

What was a rattlesnoak root doing here, inside Yuk's head?

Hercufleas trembled. His hand twitched to the sword by his side. The rattleroot raised its head to strike.

Above Hercufleas, the octopanzee-thing tossed a gleaming thread down at his feet.

'*Climb, up to me! Up here, to safety!*'

Hercufleas focused on the rattleroot. He might be in danger, but he wasn't about to trust the creature above him. It was part of Yuk, after all.

The octopanzee-thing closed its one eye and sighed. '*So you wish to die? Well, what a shame. I thought I'd found someone to save Yuk's brain.*'

'What?' Hercufleas looked up.

And the rattleroot struck.

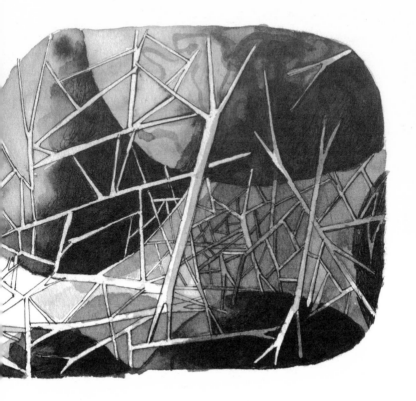

37

Greta climbed up Yuk's earlobe, ignoring the disgusting toffee-coloured wax that smeared on her hands. Finally she stood on the giant's mossy head. The world pitched and swayed beneath her as Yuk turned his head this way and that, guzzling the Tumberfolk one by one. Throat raw, heart pounding, she made her way towards the tree sprouting from his skull.

The rattlesnoak's leaves were blood red, and its spindly branches swayed black against the starry sky. At the tips of them, seed pods shook like maracas. Around the trunk, rattleroots coiled and hissed. Greta took a cautious step forward, and saw tiny silhouettes leaping up and down on the leaves above. She waved at them. The fleamily waved back.

'We're being rescued!'

'By that girl who kidnapped Hercufleas!'

'Have you seen him anywhere?'

Greta didn't answer.

She ran for the trunk, green scarf streaming in the wind, swinging her axe as she went.

Hercufleas whipped his sword up as the rattleroot lunged. M sliced the thing off at the head, and the root fell down dead. He wiped its poison from the blade and looked up at the octopanzee-thing above him.

'What did you mean?' he said, jumping up to balance on the thread beside it. 'Why does Yuk's brain need rescuing?'

The creature blinked its one eye. It mouth hung open, a grey thread dangling out. Then it began to babble excitedly.

'*At last! We're saved! What a foolish mistake I made . . . You're not a germ! Now I'm sure. You're the opposite, aren't you? The cure!*'

'Cure?' said Hercufleas, but the octopanzee-thing didn't answer. It swung from thread to thread, deeper into the brain. Hercufleas jumped after it. 'Come back! Hey!'

'*I suppose I should explain,*' the creature said as it went. '*I'm a noggin: guardian of Yuk's brain. Noggins connect his*

219

thoughts together . . . But we are being held prisoner. Now you have come to set us free! You can fight the dreadful tree!'

The Noggin stopped talking and shook hands with Hercufleas eight times. The little creature blinked its grey eye and gave a grey smile, showing grey teeth.

'Tree? Do you mean . . . that rattlesnoak on his head?' Hercufleas asked the noggin.

'Don't worry, I'll tell you everything. But before we can begin . . . we really ought to go inside. There'll be more rattleroots coming. We must hide!'

Turning round, Hercufleas saw the noggin was right: rattleroots were slithering towards them from every direction. The noggin's eight hands tugged Hercufleas back to a hiding place, a part of the web where thousands of strands met together, forming a tiny silken nest.

Hercufleas let himself be bundled inside. The noggin plastered its hands over his mouth as the rattleroots slithered past.

'Don't fear! We're safe here.' The noggin folded and unfolded all his arms nervously. *'I haven't been to this part of the brain, since the dreadful rattleroots came. Here, perhaps, you will be able to peek, at some of the answers that you seek . . . But why do you look so upset? Are you bothered by my rhyming couplets?'*

'It's just . . .' Hercufleas looked at the pulsing, flashing weave of threads surrounding him. 'You said you were a guardian of Yuk's brain?'

The noggin gave him an enthusiastic thumbs-up, eight times.

'Then that makes us enemies,' Hercufleas said sadly.

The noggin turned the colour of ashes. It hung its head. *'So you came here to destroy us? I suppose it must be. Go on . . . put us out of our misery . . .'*

'I tried to,' admitted Hercufleas. 'Then everything went wrong, and I fell into Yuk's nostril, and before I knew it, I was here. Now you're telling me that it's the giant who needs rescuing, and I want to know why.'

'Because he's a prisoner! Don't you see? His brain's been invaded by a rattlesnoak tree. I escaped: I'm the noggin in charge of Yuk's rhyme. But the rest have been captured for such a long time.' The noggin was so upset he broke down, weeping grey tears.

'I don't have time for crying!' Hercufleas shook the creature. 'Yuk is guzzling people, and I have to stop him! Tell me what to do. What happened here?'

The noggin looked up, blinking. *'It'll take too long to say.'* It sniffed. *'But I can tell you the story another way?'*

'Yes, yes,' said Hercufleas impatiently. 'Just hurry up!'

From the left, a rattleroot the size of a python sprang up from Yuk's hair. It swayed in the air, tongue flicking at Greta. With one swing of her axe, she lopped the head clean off. The rattleroot twitched and fell down dead. Three more roots slithered up from the right. They were stumps before they could even strike.

Greta held her axe the way a painter holds a brush, the way a sculptor holds a chisel. She wasn't a woodcutter, but an artist. She swung in sweeping arcs, slices, uppercuts. Dead rattleroots thumped the floor around her and she walked on towards the tree.

'Don't make it angry!' called Pin from the branches.

'It's not angry,' Greta answered. 'It's afraid.' Axe ready, she reached up towards the branches. 'Come on, everyone! Time to go!'

Hopping from the branches one after the other came the fleamily. They clustered together on her hand.

'Let's get out of here!' Greta called.

Min pointed behind her. 'Watch out!'

Greta jumped forward, dodging another rattleroot. It lunged past her, and she spun round and lopped off its head. Another two rose up. She cut them down too. But for every one she killed, another two took its place.

Soon there would be too many of them.

She cut the heads off another five rattleroots, but ten more sprouted up to attack. They lunged at Greta from different angles, and her axe spun like a deadly windmill. Nine rattleroots died, but one got through – it knocked the axe from her hand and she fell back with a cry. The snake head lunged forward, hissing. Greta saw the pink inside of its mouth, the flicking black tongue, the teeth like crescent moons.

38

Inside Yuk's head, Hercufleas hopped around the noggin's nest impatiently. He wanted answers, but the stupid creature was making him what looked like a meal – a meal of noodles, made up of various threads from Yuk's brain. The noggin had carefully chosen them from around its nest, tugging individual threads free from the web. It sniffed at them, nodded and plonked the whole tangled mess at Hercufleas's feet. It looked a little like grey spaghetti.

'*Tuck in!*' said the noggin.

'I'm not eating that!' Hercufleas snapped. 'Just tell me about Yuk.'

The noggin blinked irritably. '*It might not look like much of a treat, but to understand, first you must eat!*'

Hercufleas started to protest, at which the noggin

picked up a strand of spaghetti and shoved it in his mouth –

> *– The high wind tickles your hair*
> *and your belly rumbles like a storm.*
> *Far down, the soup makes noise.*
> *You like that. Noisy food is wriggly fresh.*
> *Which one to guzzle next? Which one looks juicy?*
> *You pick up one by its ankle – old and wrinkly, with*
> *a gold key around its neck. You open your mouth.*
> *In it goes, down it goes, wriggling all the way*
> *down to your belly. Yum yum.*
> *A beautiful white bird pecks your ankle.*
> *You pluck it up and guzzle it too.*
> *'YUM,' you say. 'TASTE LIKE CHICKEN.'*
> *Then you get your straw and start to suck*
> *up the Tumberfolk again –*

– and Hercufleas spat out the brain spaghetti. He was back in the noggin's nest.

'That was . . . I was *Yuk*,' he gasped, feeling sick. 'I just ate Mayor Witz! I ate Artifax! They're gone . . . Artifax . . .'

The noggin grasped him with eight hands and

shook him. '*It was just a recent memory! I gave it so that you could see: what Yuk is now . . . and what he used to be.*'

The creature offered up another noodle of memory-spaghetti. More memories? Hercufleas gagged. He could still feel poor Artifax wriggling in his stomach . . . But the noggin fixed him with a pleading stare. Closing his eyes, he slurped it up –

– The sky is a pale pink above the mountains,
but night still holds fast here upon the Waste.
You stand, swaying in the dark, looking out on the hills.
The emptiness. There is much work to do before sunrise.
Forest to plant, marshes to dredge,
meadows to seed, rivers to –

– and Hercufleas came back to himself again. He sat there, trying to understand the memory he had just experienced. Across from him, the noggin watched intently.

'Yuk was a green giant!' Hercufleas whispered. 'Like in the legend Greta told me.'

The noggin nodded. '*If I had told you, you wouldn't believe. Words wouldn't do: you had to see.*'

'But then why is . . . ?' Hercufleas shook his head, reached forward and stuffed the rest of the memories in his mouth. They whirled through him, one after the next –

– You step back, your work done.
All night you worked, sowing life upon the Waste.
Now the sun is coming –

– the first beams touch upon the earth,
and your wildflowers bud and bloom lavender-purple,
blossom-pink, amaranth-red –

– silently you gaze out at the Waste.
The forests surge up in the sunlight –

– you lay down upon the ground. You are tired.
Time to sleep, while the forests grow over you –

– Hercufleas leaped up, trembling all over.

'The tree on Yuk's head,' he said. 'It's a rattlesnoak. A seed fell on his head, and the roots grew into his brain.'

The noggin nodded. '*The roots invaded him while he snoozed. Now they control his every move.*'

Hercufleas looked out of the nest. Above them was the roof of Yuk's skull, like an upturned basin. Spreading from where the basin plug should be, a knotted twist of thousands of rattleroots wound down into the giant's brain.

The noggin pointed, and now Hercufleas could make out scores of other noggins among the threads. Their hands, Hercufleas saw, twanged the strands of Yuk's brain, as if it was a guitar or a harp. As their eight hands plucked, they sent out flashes of light which were the giant's thoughts.

But coiled like a python around each noggin was a rattleroot.

The poor creatures were like puppets on strings. To make Yuk move, speak or even blink, the rattlesnoak simply tightened its grip around the required noggin and forced it to send out the necessary commands.

'The rattlesnoak's what you must fight,' said the creature beside him solemnly. *'It has an enormous appetite. It makes Yuk guzzle constantly. If you could set the noggins free . . .'*

Hercufleas didn't need to hear any more. He drew *m* from his side and leaped from the nest.

39

The rattleroot's fangs gleamed as it lunged for Greta. Then a dozen black specks hopped onto its head – the fleamily. They all bit down together, and the rattleroot hissed in pain, twisting in the air. Seizing her chance, Greta scooped up her axe and lopped the snake head off. The root went rigid as a stick and fell on her lap, poisonous sap dribbling from its severed neck. She stared down at the tiny creatures that had just saved her life.

'Bleugh!' said Burp, hopping about and spitting. 'Rattlesnoak sap tastes disgusting.'

A second flea hopped down beside the first. 'Be careful, everyone!' Min cried. 'Resist any urge to slither about and be evil! Remember, you are what you eat.'

'Yesssssssss, Min,' said Dot. She shook her head. 'I mean, yes.'

Pin hopped onto Greta's shoulder. 'We'll provide a distraction while you chop down the trunk. Kill those rattleroots at the source, it's the only way we'll escape!'

Greta blinked stupidly at the limp root in her lap.

'Quick!' Min nipped her hard. 'Get chopping!'

Jolted by the bite, Greta scooped up her axe, scrambling to her feet. Suddenly the air was full of whizzing black smudges. The fleamily were everywhere, taunting the rattleroots, then hopping away from their lunges. Tittle star-jumped, Itch somersaulted, Jot did the double-pike-cross-split-topsy-turvy manoeuvre. The rattleroots tied themselves up in hissing, writhing knots.

'Hurry!' said Min. 'We can't keep this up forever!'

Greta looked at the thick trunk. She raised her axe and swung it into the tree. *THUNK*. Green sap hissed from the gash in the bark, but it was only the tiniest nick. It would take another hundred strokes to bring the rattlesnoak down.

THUNK. Ninety-nine. *THUNK*. Ninety-eight. *THUNK*.

Inside Yuk's brain, Hercufleas leaped from thread to shining thread. He gritted his teeth. His sword gleamed in his hand and his plan was keen in his head. He had to free the noggins, fast. Who knew how many Tumberfolk had followed Mayor Klare and Mrs Lorrenz down into Yuk's belly?

He crept up behind the first rattleroot. With one slice from *m*, it dropped off the noggin like loose ribbons on an unwrapped present.

'*I'm free!*' gasped the noggin, who introduced itself as Vocabulary. '*Liberated! Unchained! Emancipated!*'

Hercufleas grinned, flexed his powerful legs and jumped up, beheading another two rattleroots and freeing two more noggins, who told him their names were Optimism and Pessimism.

'*I always knew this day would come!*' one cried.

'*Bet it won't last,*' muttered the other.

On Hercufleas went, slicing dozens of rattleroots, freeing dozens of noggins. He freed Empathy (who began to weep for the dead rattleroot at its feet), Philanthropy (who began to help other noggins escape) and Apathy (who yawned, shrugged and carried on doing nothing).

Slowly the rattlesnoak began to lose control of Yuk. Hercufleas freed two noggins called Yawn and Stretch, and outside the giant stopped guzzling to yawn and stretch, as if waking up from the longest sleep. He freed Vomit, and suddenly Miss Witz and Artifax, floundering in Yuk's stomach acid, found themselves puking back up his throat. They spewed out into the air, reeking, clothes and feathers half digested, but alive.

Now, all around Yuk's brain, noggins chattered to each other, and bright white lights pulsed back and forth along the threads between them as their hands plucked the strings. Hercufleas hurdled over the next rattleroot, slicing it to pieces.

'What's your name?' he said to the noggin he'd just freed.

'Grab,' was the answer.

'Grab?' Hercufleas thought for a moment. Then he grinned. 'Grab? Listen, I've got an idea.'

Outside Yuk's head, the battle raged too. The fleamily jumped and somersaulted, dodging the rattleroots, but slowly they were being beaten back to the tree's trunk. Again and again Greta hefted her axe in the air and struck the rattlesnoak's trunk.

THUNK!

The seed pods in the branches shivered and shook. Greta swung again.

THUNK!

'Hurry!' Pin cried, as the fleas were pressed back and back. 'Hurry, child!'

THUNK! The bark was too tough. It would take Greta dozens more strokes to bring the rattlesnoak down. Unless . . .

She readied one last swing, and struck with all her might. For Mama and Papa and Wuff. For everyone.

THUNK! The axe quivered in the trunk, still only halfway through. Hot tears coursed down her cheeks. No good. They were out of time. The fleamily had nowhere left to jump: the writhing rattleroots had them completely surrounded.

Greta knew this was the end. But instead of fear, a different feeling filled her – surrender. Soon it would all be over. All the hurt and heartache, all the suffering and struggling, it was all about to fall away to nothingness.

All she had to do was give up.

She wanted to give up.

To feel nothing.

40

Greta had always imagined death would come silently, but this was deafening. An ear-splitting *CRUNCH*, then a wet snapping sound, like a million teeth sinking into a million apples and each biting off a chunk—

Every single rattleroot around her writhed in the air and fell down dead.

Leaves and twigs rained down on her, snagging in her hair. The house-hat fell at her feet, a crumpled ruin of velvet and broken glass. Greta ducked and whirled around – where the rattlesnoak had been, there was now a jagged stump. The tree trunk was being borne up into the night sky, carried away by Yuk's enormous hand.

The giant had reached up and grabbed the rattlesnoak from his own head.

Greta watched, dumbfounded, as he pulverised the

tree into splinters and brushed the whole mess from his palm.

'Are we alive?' murmured Dot.

Greta looked at the fleas and shrugged.

'I think so . . .' Min began, then they all were tipped forward, sliding down Yuk's forehead into his cupped hands. Greta lay there dazed, Yuk's mossy palm rough against her cheek. She scrambled to her feet and stared up at him. She wanted to face him without fear before he guzzled her.

Then Yuk spoke.

'You must hate me,' he said. His voice sounded strange. Softer. He wasn't bellowing any more. 'You must hate me more than anything.'

Greta nodded, but it wasn't true. She felt nothing at all. Just cold. Like she had died already.

'Hurry up and guzzle me,' she said.

'I am sorry,' said Yuk. 'But once again, Greta, I must do something painful to you. I am not going to let you give up. I am going to make you live.'

Greta looked into his eyes, the colour of rotten milk. She stared at his swampy black mouth and skin rough as bark and thorn-bush eyebrows. He was still Yuk. Still the giant who had killed her parents and terrorised her town. And yet, somehow, he was not the same. He had changed.

Yuk looked away from them to face the dawn, and at that moment the sun burst up from behind the ruined church of Saint Katerina on the Hill.

'Ahh,' he said. 'The sun.'

And as Greta watched, the light changed him. Dead vines and rattleroots clinging to his body fell away. Rippling fields of summer grass sprouted from his skin.

Poppies bloomed from the wounds the Tumberfolk had given him. His eyes were suddenly blue. His beard and hair turned the million rich hues of a forest in autumn. Yuk had transformed in front of her eyes.

'You're a green giant,' Greta breathed.

'Once,' the green giant said, his eyes looking somewhere far away. He glanced down at the remains of the rattlesnoak at his feet. 'And then I was done with planting forests, and like all my kind, I slept. And while I dreamed, the weeds began to choke the life from the garden I had made.'

'You mean rattlesnoaks?' said Greta. 'And bramble-strangle and pine-needlers?'

'I do,' said the giant. 'And one of them wriggled its roots into my head and made me a monster.'

Bending down to the riverbank, he let Greta step from his hand. The Tumberfolk were there too, in their sopping wet clothes, staring up at the giant silently.

'Farewell,' he said to them.

'Wait!' Greta called to him.

The giant paused, the summer grass on his chest ripening in the morning sun. Sparrows flitted around his hair, collecting dead rattleroot twigs for nests. A host of questions flew up from Greta like the birds.

'What just happened to you? Why are you different? What changed?'

'I am not the one to answer you,' the green giant said, stepping from the river to the woodn't. Just before he vanished into the trees, he picked an enormous bogey – like a green bowling ball – from his nose and flicked it to the ground. It crashed into the reeds, flecking Greta with mud.

'Don't flick bogeys at me!' she roared at him. 'Tell me what you mean! Where are you going? Come back!'

Scowling, she kicked the bogey as hard as she could with her clogs. It cracked like a nut and split into two halves. Within the hard crust was a gooey green centre, and there, suspended like a prehistoric insect stuck in sap . . .

Impossible.

'Noggins and nostrils,' Hercufleas groaned. 'What just happened?'

Greta began to cry. She didn't understand why Yuk had changed, but she knew who had caused it.

'You saved us,' she told Hercufleas, hot tears running down her cheeks. She plucked him from the stringy snot with her fingers.

'I did?' Hercufleas rubbed his head. 'Are you sure?'

And holding him in her hands, Greta turned to show him: the Tumberfolk sprawled by the riverbank; Mayor Witz and Artifax, covered in vomit but alive; Yuk vanishing through the trees. His fleamily hopping with joy and waving at him.

'And me,' Greta whispered. 'You saved me too.'

Hercufleas looked into her odd-coloured eyes and smiled.

'What do we do now?' she asked.

'Catch those happy tears,' he told her. 'Stick the kettle on the stove. I think everyone could do with a pot of nettle tea.'

41

Tumber was saved, but so much had been lost. Homes could be rebuilt and rubble cleared, but how did you mend the sorrow and silence? Those things will not be healed by anything but time, and time works at its own pace and will not be rushed.

The green giant came back to Tumber in the months that followed. Where else could he go? He was alone, and the other green giants were still sleeping, lost out there among the trees. Mayor Witz put him to work clearing rubble, and among the dead streets he spread what life he had to give: wildflowers, autumn grass and fruit trees.

He looked so different to Yuk, and was so gentle, that the Tumberfolk soon thought of him as a different creature altogether. Pulling the rattlesnoak from his head had torn out many of his memories, too, so that he could not remember his own name, only that it started with a Y. Mayor Witz suggested he choose a new name, but the green giant insisted that name could not just spring out of nothing, but needed time to grow. So it was that the Tumberfolk called him Y to begin with, and every month the green giant chose the next letter to add to his name.

Time passed, and Y became Yân, and then Yânar, and Tumber came slowly back to life.

The fleamily remained in the town too, for a while. Min and Pin wanted to leave as soon as possible – after all, they had a new hero to take back to Avalon and hire out at Happily Ever Afters, which they could run themselves now Mr Stickler was gone.

'I'll have the fleas draw up a contract as soon as we're back,' Min gabbled to Hercufleas. 'I'll hire you out for giant-slayings and rescues – and I think we should talk merchandise too. Just think! Yuk action dolls! Toothpicks in the shape of your sword! Giant bogey-green gobstoppers, with a toy flea inside! Obviously we'll have to put "choking hazard" on the packet . . .'

But though the fleamily talked about starting up a new business hiring heroes, and repairing the house-hat, and maybe even adding a jacuzzi to the bathroom, somehow they kept putting off leaving Tumber. There was just so much to do.

Itch, Titch and Tittle typed up a whole new library of books for the school. Burp and Slurp started up a flea circus to entertain the Tumberfolk, tightrope-walking across two broom handles connected with cotton thread. Dot painted the nails of the roost-wives with tiny frescoes: portraits and still lives and Petrossian landscapes. She got so good that people started to call her Leonarda da Tinchi.

Everyone had a job, and when they sat together in the evenings and recited *The Plea of the Flea* they were truly thankful to be together. They laughed and jumped and joked, just like before. There was only one thing missing: the fleamily needed a home.

It wasn't just that the house-hat was a wreck. It had been ruined long before Yuk – by Stickler. The fleamily were never quite able to enjoy their pantry of exotic blood, or the boingy-boing room, after finding out their host had paid for it all by hiring out villains as well as heroes.

At first Hercufleas suggested they should live with Greta, but she never built her house of logs, the one she had spoken of when they were out in the Waste.

Life was hard for her for a long time. Although she had helped save Tumber, Greta could never be saved from her own past. It was always there. Her parents were gone, and they would always be gone, and every day hurt.

But Hercufleas had given her a future, and though it was not quite a Happily Ever After, still Greta filled it with what happiness she could.

There were the evenings she spent with Mayor Witz, eating sweet beetroot pies, drinking nettle tea and telling stories in the warm light of the stove. Evenings that reminded her of her parents.

There was Artifax, with his soft white feathers that she stroked, and his loving purple eyes. Artifax, who reminded her so much of Wuff.

There were the long days she spent up on Yânarik's head, which had grown into a meadow of sage and camomile. Watching the Earth stretch endlessly away to the west and endlessly return from the east. Sometimes she took her axe up there, and other tools too, though what she was making she never told anyone – except Hercufleas.

Hercufleas.

As always, he was the voice whispering hope in her ear. The one constant on her shoulder. It was Hercufleas who saved Greta, again and again, whenever grief threatened her. He never stopped being her hero.

Six months after the battle of Tumber, Greta rode Artifax out into the woodn't. The roost-wife who saw her go said she crossed the bridge without dropping her tears into the river. When Hercufleas heard that, he knew she wasn't ever coming back.

No one knew where she went. The cinderwikk men said it was to Avalon, to tell the truth about Prince Xin and Ugor. The cossacks shook their heads: Greta had gone to the Sorrows, to try to find a way to bring life back to the salt lakes. No, clucked the roost-wives, she went back to the Waste, to live with Sir Klaus and the Mousketeers.

Hercufleas did not know who was right. On the morning that Greta left, she didn't say goodbye. When he woke, still snuggled in her green scarf, it lay draped on the ground. She hadn't even left a note – just a single drop of her blood in a thimble, there beside him. Hours later, after he had searched all through the town calling her name, he came back and drank it down. It was sweet and full of sorrow, leaving a lump in his throat for hours. But for the first time, the bitterness had gone.

That night in his dreams he saw a fierce bramble-haired girl riding a bird through the trees, searching for the giants, green and great as cathedrals, who lay dreaming deep in the forests.

He saw her reach them, though it was many years in the future and she had grown old. He watched her wake the giants and lead them back to Tumber, to find their lost brother who had wandered off while they slept. And just before Hercufleas woke, he saw the green giant – whose name had grown so long it would fill a book – reunited with his family, and in that moment Greta's grief finally left her forever.

But in truth, where Greta went was known only to her, for no two hearts beat alike nor break alike, and so each must be mended in its own way.

'I wish I'd told her the truth,' Hercufleas said to Mayor Witz, a month after Greta left. 'I never explained about the Black Death.'

Mayor Witz polished her gold key. 'What about it?' she asked innocently.

Hercufleas sighed. 'You were wrong,' he admitted. 'When I got there – inside that chest where it was – I saw the truth. Yes, it would have destroyed Yuk. But it wouldn't have stopped there. It would have carried on killing – on and on. First the Tumberfolk, then Petrossia, then the world. Sir Klaus told me . . . Only evil can come of the Black Death. So I didn't drink it. I didn't take its power.'

He expected surprise, but she just looked crafty as the fox on the handle of her walking stick. 'Dear little flea,' she said. 'By the time you reached the Black Death, you didn't need its power.'

Hercufleas looked at her. He thought back to that time, long ago, when Mayor Witz had sat knitting Greta's scarf and his destiny into being.

'You never wanted me to bring the Black Death back,' he realised. 'But why did you send us all that way, if you knew it was for nothing?'

'I knew no such thing,' Mayor Witz answered crossly. 'And some power *did* come back with you.'

Hercufleas groaned. Mayor Witz was getting forgetful in her old age. 'I already told you,' he said. 'I didn't take—'

'I did not say the power was in *you*,' Mayor Witz interrupted.

Hercufleas frowned. 'It wasn't?'

She shook her head. 'It was in Greta.'

'*Greta?*'

'Greta.' She nodded. 'When she left here, her heart

was cold and despairing. All our hearts were. She came back carrying a flicker of hope. Like a tinderfly within her heart. And look at the fire it sparked. Even in you.'

Hercufleas shook his head. The wily old babushka was right.

'We're all fleas feeding off of a creature called Hope,' he grinned, remembering Sir Klaus, and suddenly he knew that Greta would be fine, wherever she went and whatever she did.

42

On the day Hercufleas and his fleamily left Tumber, the whole town turned out to say goodbye. So many sad tears were cried that the nettle tea was ruined and the fleas had to wear wellingtons. Mayor Witz stepped up to an enormous object in the centre of the town, hidden under a white sheet.

'Big Things are easy to remember,' she told the town. 'Big Things almost never get lost. It would be very strange, for example, if tomorrow you saw someone walking down the street, scratching their head and saying to themselves, "Now where did I put Avalon?" Avalon is a Big Thing, you see.

'It's the Small Things that tend to get forgotten. They are always slipping from our heads, like coins down the back of an armchair. It would not be very strange at all, for example, if tomorrow you saw someone by the side of the road, scratching their heads and saying to themselves, "Where are my scopical glasses?" or "What's the name of that little dot on top of the letter i?"'

'Just so you know, it's called a tittle,' said Tittle.

'Questions like these will always be asked,' Mayor Witz continued, 'because people have a habit of forgetting about the Small Things. But just because something (or someone) is small doesn't mean they aren't important. They can still do stupendous, awe-inspiring, heroic things. And that's why we must remember Hercufleas.'

With that, she unveiled the statue in the town square.

A bronze flea, with the inscription:

Until the flea bit, the child wouldn't fight.
Until the child fought, the axe wouldn't chop.
Until the axe chopped, the tree wouldn't fall.
Until the tree fell, the giant wouldn't wake.
Until the giant woke, the nightmare couldn't end.
And all from the bite of a flea.

The crowd burst into applause, then looked at Hercufleas. Now it was his turn to make a speech. But he just stood there, looking at his statue.

After a while, the Tumberfolk began to get nervous. Was something wrong? Was the statue not grand enough? Should it have been made from marble instead of bronze? Was his nose too stubby? Were his spines too spiky? That was it, wasn't it? His spines were definitely too spiky, they had thought the same thing.

'Do you . . . like it?' asked Mayor Witz tentatively.

Hercufleas looked up with a sad smile. 'I'm honoured,' he said to her. Then he turned to the Tumberfolk. 'But I don't want a statue.'

Mayor Witz frowned. 'But—'

'I'm not a hero,' said Hercufleas firmly. 'I'm just a flea

who lost his fleamily and then found them again. A flea who found a best friend and then lost her.'

The mayor spread her hands. 'What would you have us do?'

Hercufleas thought for a while. He looked up at Yânariko, standing high above them.

'Plant an everpine seed here,' he called up, cupping his hands at his mouth and yelling hard as he could. 'So they will always remember: big things come from small beginnings!'

And that is exactly what the green giant did. He planted the seed, and the Tumberfolk saw it grow tall. When it was big enough, they wrote the names of everyone who had been lost upon the leaves, starting with Natalya and Nicholas and Wuff. All through spring and summer they lay upon the branches, whispering to each other in the breeze. In autumn, each loss withered and blew away.

'Come on then, all of you,' said Min. 'It's a long way to Avalon, and we've been here far too long already.'

But Hercufleas shook his head. 'We're not going to Avalon.'

'We're not?' said Pin.

'No,' said Hercufleas, taking his fleamily's hands and forming them into a circle. 'We need a new home.'

'If not Avalon, then where?' said Min.

'And who will our host be?' said Pin.

Hercufleas grinned. 'You'll never know unless you jump. Ready? On three.'

The fleas looked at each other nervously.

'One . . .'

Were they ready? Of course they weren't! What was Hercufleas going on about?

'Two . . .'

But he looked at them with such belief that the question no longer seemed to matter.

'Three!'

The Tumberfolk never saw them again.

Epilogue

The fleamily landed on a hillside meadow of chamomile and sage, beside an old hollowed-out tree stump. It had tall square windows carved into the sides and a blood-red door with a brass knocker and a tiny sign, painted with an eyelash. It said 'Stump Cottage'.

The fleamily stood staring at it.

'Where are we?' said Dot.

'On Yânariko's head,' said Hercufleas.

The others looked down at their feet in amazement.

'Look,' said Hercufleas, pointing at the supplies piled by the tree stump. 'We've got elastic bands, to make a new boingy-boing room. Pints of blood to put in the pantry. Matchsticks and candles and a cloth we can cut into blankets, and even a box of tinderflies we can breed for fires!'

'You made all of this?' Min gasped, looking around the stump. 'It must be ten times the size of the hat house!'

'Greta built it,' Hercufleas said. 'Before she left. Yânariko knows. He's offered to be our new host. We can stay on him for as long as we like. All he asks in return is for us to make sure that nothing nasty plants itself on him ever again. We'll be like his gardeners, uprooting any nasty weeds.' He stared at them all, hopping about with nerves. 'What do you think?'

The fleamily looked around them, then back to Stump Cottage. And they burst out laughing.

'Unbe*flea*vable!' said Itch.

'*Parasitic*ulous!' said Titch.

'*Pest*itively brilliant!' said Burp.

Hercufleas smiled. He joined the others in celebrating. They did star jumps, and somersaults, and double-pike-cross-split-topsy-turvy manoeuvres, leaping through the meadow towards home.

Acknowledgements

Sometimes, words are like fleas: pesky little things that won't stay where I want them to. Hopping all over the page. Itching and irritating. Leaving me feeling faint.

At one point, the words in this book grew into an enormous swarm that I just didn't know what to do with.

Lucky for me, I've got a crack team of Pest Control.

Charlie Sheppard, Eloise Wilson and Chloe Sackur at Andersen – thank you for your wisdom and imagination. You make my books the best they can be! Eve Warlow and Sarah Kimmelman – thank you for your invites and organising. Small books get overlooked sometimes. You make sure mine get noticed.

Talya Baker, my copy-editor – thank you for your keen eye and clarity. Peter Cottrill – thank you for bringing the world of the story to life. Kate Grove – thank you for your direction, design and mad Photoshopping skillz.

Claire Lawrence – thanks for entering and winning my Really Tiny Story Competition. I hope you like your characters!

Becky Bagnell, my agent – thank you for your belief and judgement. You are my champion!

And Mum – as ever, you're the best.

Super Fleas

In 1938, a comic book was published about a superhero with a red cape and a big S on his chest. This superhero could leap over twenty-storey buildings. He was super strong. Bullets bounced off his skin.

You know the guy I'm talking about, right?

Thing is, I could never figure why there's still so much fuss about him. You see, he's not that special. There are super-strong, mega-leaping, tough-as-nails superheroes everywhere. It's just that nobody notices them. Because they're also teeny-tiny.

You know the bugs I'm talking about, right?

At first, I couldn't believe fleas were such powerful parasites. But the more I researched them, the more amazed I was . . .

Fleas are so difficult to squash because their skin is made of a hard material called chitin. It's like wearing a natural suit of armour.

We humans have a guy called Zsolt Sinka, from Hungary, who can pull aeroplanes with his teeth. Pretty impressive, right? Wrong – because a flea his size could pull the equivalent of 218 jumbo jets. Sorry, Mr Sinka.

When fleas jump, their legs accelerate them at 150g – that's 150 times the force of gravity, and over 23 times that of the world's most extreme roller coaster. And they can do that 30,000 times without taking a break. (I wonder who measured that, by the way? Did they use tally marks?)

If fleas were human-sized, we might find ourselves in a lot of trouble. Especially since they can drink 15 times their bodyweight in blood.

Don't worry too much, though – because of how gravity works, fleas only have such incredible abilities because they are so small. If they grew much bigger, they'd lose all their powers.

Size, you see, is sort of like a flea's Kryptonite.

And sadly, fleas tend to be more villainous than heroic. They've even been used by criminals like Lydia Banot, who in 1996 was jailed for eight years after trying to blackmail Harrods, the famous department store. Banot threatened to release a plague of fleas in the designer-clothing department unless the shop gave her millions of pounds.

Unbe*flea*vable!

About the Author

Sam Gayton grew up in Kent with a cat called Archibald, a dog called Ruby, a bunch of humans, and a ghost called Kevin. He spent his days playing with Lego, designing new and extremely complicated board games, and making comics with his friend Loo Loo.

When he had a spare moment, he wrote stories.

They usually contained lots of dinosaurs and explosions (as all good stories should). He started thousands over the years, but he never finished any of them. He gave up, and his stories ended up stuffed into boxes and dumped in the attic.

Poor old stories! There they sat, year after year, heaped with the dust and the spiders and Kevin the ghost, waiting for their endings. Probably they ended up haunting Sam, because a long time later, when he had grown up and decided to be a teacher, he somehow found himself writing stories again.

And this time, he didn't give up on them.

Sam still loves Lego, board games and comics. But now he also loves drinking tea (milk, no sugar), eating pizza (pepperoni, extra cheese), and wondering how long he would survive a zombie apocalypse (probably about 14 minutes).

@sam_gayton

www.samgayton.com

THE SNOW

MERCHANT

SAM GAYTON

ILLUSTRATED BY CHRIS RIDDELL

Lettie Peppercorn lives in a house on stilts near the
wind-swept coast of Albion. Nothing incredible has
ever happened to her, until one winter's night.
The night the Snow Merchant comes.
He claims to be an alchemist – the greatest that ever
lived – and in a mahogany suitcase, he carries his
newest invention.
It is an invention that will change
Lettie's life – and the world –
forever. It is an invention
called snow.

'A delightful debut . . . full of action
and invention' *Sunday Times*

'A germ of JK and a pinch
of Pullman' *TES*

9781783441778 £6.99 Paperback

Lilliput

SAM GAYTON

'Have you heard of the tale that's short and tall? There's an island in the world where everything is small!'

Lily is three inches tall, her clothes are cut from handkerchiefs and stitched with spider silk. She was kidnapped and is kept in a birdcage. But tonight she is escaping.

Join Lily as she travels over rooftops, down chimneys and into chocolate shops on a journey to find the one place in the world where she belongs . . . Home.

'An undertaking of which Swift himself would have approved'
Irish Times

9781849397483 £6.99 Paperback